Amalie Berlin lives with her family and her critters in Southern Ohio, and writes quirky and independent characters for Mills & Boon Medical Romance. She likes to buck expectations with unusual settings and situations, and believes humour can be used powerfully to illuminate the truth—especially when juxtaposed against intense emotions. Love is stronger and more satisfying when your partner can make you laugh through the times when you don't have the luxury of tears.

Also by Amalie Berlin

Taming Hollywood's Ultimate Playboy
Challenging the Doctor Sheikh
Dante's Shock Proposal
The Prince's Cinderella Bride
The Rescue Doc's Christmas Miracle
Back in Dr Xenakis' Arms

Scottish Docs in New York miniseries

Their Christmas to Remember
Healed Under the Mistletoe

Discover more at millsandboon.co.uk.

THEIR CHRISTMAS TO REMEMBER

AMALIE BERLIN

MILLS & BOON

First published in Great Britain 2018
by Mills & Boon, an imprint of HarperCollins*Publishers*
1 London Bridge Street, London, SE1 9GF

Large Print edition 2019

© 2018 Amalie Berlin

ISBN: 978-0-263-07828-2

FLINTSHIRE SIR Y FFLINT	
C29 0000 1197 078	
MAGNA	£16.99

ified
ent. For
green.

Dedicated to my mom, Jeanne,
the world's best nurse.
She always goes above and beyond
for those in her care.

CHAPTER ONE

DR. ANGELICA CONLEY knocked once before pushing into the room of her very first patient at Sutcliffe Memorial Hospital almost a year after that first treatment in Emergency. A patient she'd been saddened to see readmitted earlier in the week.

"Hi, Jenna." She wasn't Jenna's doctor now, she'd just had the sad duty of discovering and diagnosing Jenna's original nephroblastoma, which had recurred after six months of remission. Jenna was now under the care of a pediatric oncologist and the Scottish pediatric surgeon who unknowingly set Angel's imagination on fire. At least she hoped he didn't know but, considering the way women seemed to fall at his feet, he probably at least suspected. She was alive, after all. It was one of the only things she had in common with her colleagues. In almost every other way, she stood apart from them, an oddity who didn't fit in to the Manhattan scene, and never could.

She really should've known that from the start—she'd had three decades to write it into her DNA, but she'd still fallen for the fantasy that things could be different here, that who she was and where she'd come from wouldn't matter. But within three days at her first New York job, her past had come back to bite her, which was how she'd ended up at Sutcliffe. Fortunate, probably, but still…

Being human was the only thing she had in common with her colleagues and being subject to the emotions that came with it. Like humiliation. If the serial Scottish flirt hadn't sorted out her pesky reaction to him yet, she just had to hang in there until January and she'd be far enough away it would no longer matter what he or the rest of her New York colleagues felt about the Kentucky bumpkin who'd taken the turnip truck to medical school. She'd never hear them laughing from eight hundred miles away.

And in Atlanta, no one knew her or her history. Especially not old boyfriends she'd once been young and foolish enough to share with. Turned out New York really wasn't that big if you shared the same profession.

But this was about Jenna. Not about Angel's own problems. Or the Scotsman.

Although it was hard to fake a smile in the face of bad news, that didn't mean Angel couldn't try and put the twelve-year-old at ease, especially since she'd heard there was something more amiss today.

Jenna lay in her hospital bed, swaddled in extra blankets, the dark, sunken shadow below her brown eyes an unfortunate and telling symptom of a wasting disease along with the natural exhaustion and fear that accompanied it.

She didn't bother turning her attention to Angel, who she usually called her favorite doctor. The lack of response and her dull stare at the television could mean anything; the trauma swirling around her was as much emotional exhaustion as physical.

"I heard you're not feeling well today." Angel tried anyway, praying she had some leverage. It was only three days since surgery, and Jenna needed to eat to get better, which had been the day's report: *Jenna's refusing to eat.*

"No." The one-word answer set her alarm bells to full volume. No matter what was going on, Jenna tended to maintain a generally happy outlook, regardless of her difficult diagnosis and obstacles. Today, there wasn't even a hint of a smile on her face.

This could take a while. And that was okay. Angel's shift was over; she had time for however long her quick visit became. Her tiny, half-empty apartment wouldn't miss her.

The door to the bathroom was closed. Angel tilted her head to listen and look for light beneath, but there was nothing. "Your mom here today?"

"No." Another single word answer. Whatever was wrong, there would be no quick solve.

Angel snagged a chair and slid it up to the bedside, indicating her intention to stay. "Did she have to work?"

"No."

"Has she already left for the day?"

"No…" This time the admission came with a little quiver to her lower lip.

The weight and tightness blooming in Angel's chest had her leaning forward, trying to keep alarm from entering her voice. Something must have happened. Nothing insignificant would keep Mrs. Lindsey away from her daughter's bedside for even a day.

She took a moment and studied the girl's position in the bed. She'd considered it a hallmark of weakness and exhaustion, but since they'd started to speak, Jenna's arms had crossed over her chest. She also avoided eye contact. The teariness wasn't worry, she was *angry*. This was not the product of an emergency.

Just narrowing the options away from fear to anger eased the alarm roiling through her. Angel sat back up, allowing a deep breath. Sometimes she was glad for the survival skills her earliest education had given her. She might've been born far from any kind of city, but she could read people well enough to catch the first whiff of danger and knew when to depart before situations escalated to the need to *run*. It also came in handy in normal conversation or treating kids who really didn't want treatment.

"Where is she?"

"With Mattie." Jenna looked as far from Angel as she could then, out of the windows to the flurries blowing around in the late November chill.

Did that mean outside? "Where did they go?"

"It's his birthday," Jenna murmured, then added, "and it's on tree day this year."

The lighting of the Christmas tree at Rockefeller Center was happening today. Always the first Wednesday after Thanksgiving, which Angel had celebrated last week with the best turkey sandwich she'd ever tasted, purchased the night before from an authentic New York deli.

"Is that what he wanted for his birthday?" Hard to believe—the kid was four. Would be easier to believe if he wanted to visit the tree at the local pizza arcade.

"We always go. Every year." Jenna's voice wobbled.

Every year. Except this year she didn't get to go. This year, which had been a bad year. And this week had started with her losing one of her kidneys along with the tumor that had reached her spine with enough pressure to corrupt her balance and the ability to control her legs. Her second such surgery this year, and it promised another round of chemotherapy after Christmas. Her hair had only just gotten long enough to begin styling again.

It was a lot for a child. It would've been a lot for an adult.

"Next year you'll get to go again." Angel heard the words come out, knew it was wrong to say it—no one could promise this child she'd be alive next year—but the defeat she saw in the slope of Jenna's frail shoulders and the pain in her voice had the words flying out of Angel's mouth before that logical part of her brain kicked in. All there was in that second was the need to comfort, connecting with the part of her own soul that knew bitter disappointment and wished to soothe that hurt so hard that any heart could hear it.

"No, I won't." The softly spoken words dropped like stones in the room. "No more holidays after this year. Maybe Valentine's Day, not that any boy would want to be the Valentine of Baldy."

"Now you're just talking crazy." Angel snagged Jenna's bony hand and squeezed, and, though she'd yet to get any eye contact from the girl, took it as a small sign of hope when she didn't pull away. "You know tomorrow you're going to feel a lot more like yourself. What can I do to make *today* better?"

"Take me to the tree."

She'd been told *No* so much lately, but Angel had to say it again. "Sweet girl, you know I would do that if I could."

A chirp from the neglected laptop on Jenna's bedside table interrupted Angel's train of thought, then she remembered. "They'll broadcast it tonight, the whole ceremony with the singers and the Rockettes. We could watch it together? I'll go get us some dinner, and we'll

sit here and soak up Christmas spirit with whatever you want."

"It's not the same," Jenna grumbled. "They
do those shots from far away. They don't get up
close and look way up at the top. One time, I
even crawled below the barrier rails and almost
got to the tree before they caught me."

The tree could be leverage to get her to eat.

Sometimes she still thought like the criminals who'd raised her, and even if this was a con
that was being used for good, that pang of self-
disgust still stabbed cold into the back of her
neck for the briefest of moments. Before she
used that leverage anyway.

"What if I took my phone to Rockefeller Center and went to the base of the tree, and live
streamed it for you to watch, right from the thick
of things? You could tell me what you wanted
to see, and I'd go film that."

Jenna finally looked at her, and a little zing of
triumph negated that lance of less positive feelings about herself.

"You would?" Voice so hopeful, but her expression shouted worry this was just something
else she couldn't have. "Would you bring me a
peppermint hot cocoa and a snickerdoodle from
the cookie shop?"

Got her.

"I absolutely would do that for you. Would you do something for me if I did?"

"What?"

"Eat some lunch?" Angel phrased it like a question and pretended even to herself that she'd had no ulterior motive for visiting the little patient, that she'd have come and visited anyway because it was the kind thing to do. That was what good people did, and it was something she was working on. Might always be working on. "I'll tell them to bring up something good. You eat it, and I'll live stream the tree lighting and bring you goodies afterward."

Jenna looked for a moment as if she didn't know whether to laugh or cry, but then smiled so wide Angel could ignore the regret she should feel for her terrible adulting skills. "I will!"

She did better in her daily life and in her practice, but Jenna was special. And Angel knew a whole lot about disappointment and deprivation, which colored her actions. She might not be able to *cure* Jenna today, but she could make today better.

Angel rounded the bed to fetch the laptop, and they took a moment to link to her social media account, then checked the schedule for the tree ceremony.

"Lasses." A deep, deliciously resonant voice came from the open door behind her, announcing the arrival of the brain-scrambling Scotsman.

He did that on purpose, she was just sure of it—the man's brogue got thicker when he wanted to pour on the charm, as he apparently now did.

She was yet another weak creature who responded. Oh, she tried not to like it, and usually failed. Like right now, she failed completely to control her smile reflex. No matter how hard she willed softness and relaxation into her cheeks, they fired anyway. The best she could do was try to twist it into a rueful grimace as she made room for the surgeon.

"Jenna, my love, I'm hearing rumors you're no' eatin'." Dr. Wolfe McKeag hit the *R*s in his speech so hard they seemed to keep on rolling even after he'd moved on to lavish his attention on other words. Did he do that with his family? Dr. Lyons McKeag, his brother, worked in the ER with Angel, and he seemed to have become much more acclimatized to the sound of American vowels. And *R*s.

However Wolfe McKeag liked to live his life,

it wasn't her business. But how strange it must be to be so proud of where he came from that he'd play it up instead of hiding it completely. To not live in perpetual fear of being found out if anyone got close… She'd told one person and lost her first job. The possibility that he'd tell someone here and get her fired again always sat in the back of her mind.

Angel couldn't imagine life without that edge. Being so comfortable with herself, her past. Even a decade after removing herself entirely from the place and the people of her early life, all that came to mind when she actively tried not to think back was the lone pair of pants she'd had to wear one year.

What kind of demented designer even made camouflage-patterned corduroy? Certainly not one who had ever worn camouflage in a practical sense. Not even the stealthiest hunter could sneak up on a deer if every step announced their arrival. Not that she'd been able to shoot the deer that time she'd tried to help her father hunt when the larder ran bare.

And none of that had any bearing on her day, or the evening's tasks ahead of her. McKeag could stay here and sweet-talk Jenna all he liked, but Angel had already solved the problem. She might not have had to if she'd waited—even a twelve-year-old couldn't help but cave when McKeag came cooing.

Shooting the kid a surreptitious smile, she made her way toward the door, greeting him in passing. "Dr. McKeag."

"Dr. Conley," he returned, and she chanced a glance to find his pale blue eyes fixed on her. Just for a second. Just long enough to awaken the bitey critters in her belly. Some people had butterflies, Angel had things with teeth. And they roused so infrequently she'd have sworn they'd died off long ago, except for McKeag.

"Dr. Wolfe, I'm going to eat. Dr. Angel is going to get me peppermint cocoa and snickerdoodles."

Kid made it sound as if that was the food she'd agreed to eat...

"Dr. Angel?" he repeated.

And the bitey belly critters escaped her middle and went instead to biting and sending goosebumps down her arms. The soft hair stood on end, like an ineffective porcupine.

He really needed to never say her first name again. Ever.

"She's my Angel," Jenna said, and that was enough to bring Angel's smile back just as she ducked out of the room and into the safe, antiseptic solace of an empty corridor, where she could breathe.

Body betrayals were something she'd not miss about New York City, or about Sutcliffe. She rather preferred being cadaver-like from the neck down. It was safe. No primordial body signals to contend with meant she could devote her whole body to the list of actual, important problems she managed. Like finding a dietitian and sweet-talking her into a late lunch for Jenna.

And sorting out how to sweet-talk the dietitian before she got down there because, as well as she could read people, she lacked any skills in sweet talk.

The heavy door swung closed behind Conley, the force of the swing shoving the air and producing a wave of her scent that hit Wolfe dead on. Fruity, and something else. Not a perfume, he didn't think. Or maybe it was. There was something soft about it. Sweet. Made him think of the first breath of spring on the breeze after a long, cold winter.

A perfumer would make a killing with that scent.

Her bare skin probably smelled even better.

Everywhere. Something he'd have to be satisfied imagining—Wolfe had only a few rules, and not dating a coworker sat at the top. After a childhood drowning in the scandals of his parents, he hadn't followed his older brother across the Atlantic just to invite more drama once he got settled. Not into his life, and especially not at work. Conley was a nonstarter. No matter how fantastic she smelled. No matter how delightfully freckled her skin.

"Dr. Wolfe?"

Jenna's voice broke through the wrong direction his thoughts had taken, reminding him where he was and what he was supposed to be about. With a patient, preparing to cajole her into eating. He should be joking. Not focused on the sexy-sweet wake left behind the departing southern belle with her long *E*s and gentle cadence.

"I think I've got bad breath," he said, snapping back into the appropriate mindset as he turned back to face the young girl.

She grinned at him, her cheeks still dimpling no matter how badly her body was failing her. No matter what he'd been told, her spirit still sparkled through the veil of the sickness draped over her. "Why do you think that?"

"She left very quickly, your Angel, didn't she? And right after I got here." He lifted one brow, his best Sherlock Holmes impression.

Someone had charted a mountain, but whatever had been wrong with the girl had been a molehill. She seemed in her normal Jenna–high spirits.

He didn't mention that Conley always left quickly when he was around—that would mean he noticed. Or cared. Maybe she did that when anyone was around. He enjoyed light-hearted chatter with everyone, but, during the year since she'd arrived, he could count on one hand the number of times he'd seen Conley around anyone outside patient consultations and their irregularly scheduled department meetings for Pediatrics, which shouldn't matter to him either.

"She's in a hurry because she's going to the tree lighting tonight."

"Ah, Christmas. Gets earlier every year, doesn't it?" Earlier and more obnoxious, but Wolfe knew better than to try and explain his feelings on the holiday to a child, especially one who needed to look forward to the magic he'd heard it held but couldn't quite remember feeling. Inadequate small-talk about the holiday was the best he could do.

She argued, though with less energy. "No, it takes forever to get here."

The tree was just the official, publicly agreed as acceptable kick-off to the Lousy Season. Stores had begun pushing Christmas about the same time they began pushing Halloween. Which was when he stopped going to stores and wouldn't really resume until February. The explosion of tinsel and fairy lights that covered the city? Harder to avoid.

It was on his lips to tell her that time moved faster the older you got, but it sounded like a promise he'd love to make but couldn't. "Are you waiting for Santa?"

"No." She rolled her eyes at him and then looked at him far too closely. "Why don't you like the tree?"

He must've made a face…

"It's just a big tree," he answered, adding, "and it's cold out there."

Just as he was about to ask her about the lunch he'd heard she'd refused, and the breakfast she'd also refused, she started squirming in the bed, trying to shift up higher so that the bend of the mattress fit the bend of her body, and all the color drained from her face.

He knew that look. Pain. Kids could forget

they'd had their bodies cut open and that they weren't yet able to move freely.

"Easy…" he said, stepping in to gingerly help her into a more comfortable lean. "Don't want to pull a staple. I did a good job there, but I'd like to revisit it about as much as I'd like to go see that big silly tree."

She settled, and he watched her for a few seconds as her breathing evened out and she lost some of that worrisome pallor. "All right now?"

"I love the lighting and the tree." She sailed right past his question and got back to what *she* wanted to talk about. But the fact that she was talking at all answered his question. "We go every year."

When her little mouth twisted at the end of the statement, he knew it wasn't physical pain.

Conley had been there before him, and had done something to brighten Jenna's spirits, but he'd somehow just made her sad again.

Emotions. He wasn't good at emotions. He could generally identify them, or when there had been an emotional shift, but he wasn't good at responding. At least, he wasn't good with all the emotions that weren't amusement. He was good at that one. But even he failed to amuse when things ran too deep, too real.

Without his usual joking to fall back on, and knowing he'd not made the situation any better, it took him several seconds to come up with something resembling the proper response. "Family tradition?"

She nodded, then swiped her eyes with the arm that didn't have the IV in it. "Except this year. They're going without me."

Joking wouldn't help this. Even with his limited emotional palette, he could see that.

The location of the door through which he could escape became this presence in his mind, temptation glowing behind him. Hard to ignore. It would be so easy to say something polite, manufacture a reason to dart out and make his escape, maybe summon Conley back to cheer Jenna up again. Easy, but impossible. Good guys didn't do that kind of thing.

"Aww, lass. I'm sorry you're stuck here with the like of me this year."

She sniffed, mustering such a pitiful little smile he felt worse for wanting to leave. "I like you."

"I like you too." It seemed the thing to say. Reassuring. Maybe even putting the conversation back to one where he knew how to respond.

Then she asked, "You really don't want to go to the lighting?"

"Nah." He waved a hand, made an exaggerated face of dismissal, shook his head, played up what silliness he had in him at the moment.

Then he saw it, a little sparkle returned to her dark eyes. She tilted her head and crooned, "You wouldn't go with me if I could go?"

The playful and entirely unserious flirting of a twelve-year-old? That he could deal with. Much easier to play than try to solve problems he had no business making worse through his inadequacy. Stick with what he was good at: bodies. He was good at fixing bodies. He wasn't a neurologist, or a psychologist, although that might've been helpful when his brother had been shot. Or now, with a fragile, overwrought twelve-year-old girl.

Ruffling Jenna's short, dark hair, he teased, "That's a bit different, isn't it? I'd be goin' with you for the company. No' the silly tree."

"You would?"

"Course I would," he assured her, then, trying to make sure this was on proper ground, added, "We'd bring your whole family. And Dr. Angel."

"Dr. Angel's going to take me tonight," she

suddenly announced, voice far brighter than it had been. "And you can come with us!"

Her happy, chirruped words set his shoulders to granite, stiff and rigid enough to build on.

Was that how Conley had brightened her mood? The woman who smelled of heaven had promised to take his patient out of the hospital without a discharge order or consultation?

Surely not...

"Dr. Angel said she was taking you to Rockefeller Center tonight?" he asked, just to be sure. Always best to do your due diligence before ripping some hide off a colleague.

"Jenna, don't fib to Dr. McKeag." Angel's voice came from the door at his back, then she came into view and he looked at her fully.

Smiling. She was smiling. This was a joke?

Jenna argued, sullenness drifting into her voice as she folded her arms. "It's true. Sort of."

"Yes," Angel agreed. "But the *'sort of'* part is important. Look how red his face got."

Jenna innocently asked, "Are you embarrassed, Dr. Wolfe?"

"Angry," Angel corrected.

"I'm waiting to decide. After someone explains *'sort of'* to me."

Jenna frowned so dramatically it'd have been comical in any other situation.

"I'm going to go to the ceremony and live stream it for her, let her tell me where she wants me to film. That sort of thing," Conley explained, as if that were an everyday occurrence, nothing special.

"It'll be almost like I get to go," Jenna added, but Wolfe couldn't take his eyes off the angel in the room, living up to her name.

He couldn't stop himself from smiling either. Nurses went above and beyond all the time for their patients, but Wolfe didn't see it much in the physicians. Even in himself, which at that moment made him feel like a jerk, so the smile kind of annoyed him. It warmed his cold, anti-Christmas heart. Slightly.

Had to be relief over not having to cause drama at the hospital. "That's really—"

"My end of the deal," Angel cut in, then directed her attention back to Jenna. "Speaking of, Dietary will bring you something good any minute. And when we get finished with the tree, I'll bring you the peppermint cocoa."

"And the snickerdoodle."

"And the snickerdoodle," Angel confirmed. "I haven't forgotten."

Bribed with sweets and the ability to boss an adult around for her own amusement? Someone should teach Dr. Angel how to bargain. And maybe take lessons from Jenna.

"Dr. Wolfe is going to go with you," Jenna said.

Wolfe snapped back to the conversation. "I'm what now?"

"You said you would go with me," Jenna reminded him, sounding terribly pleased with herself. So much different from the sad little sprite she'd been earlier.

He looked at Angel to get a read on her reaction, but her carefully closed expression and the lack of any sort of verbal response told Wolfe he'd get no help from her. She wasn't even looking at him.

Did that mean she *did* or *didn't* want him to go?

Dammit. All these emotional landmines. He hated trying to sort this stuff out. He'd much rather deal with actual guts than metaphorical ones.

If he backed out now, that'd probably be insulting a colleague. As a pediatric emergency specialist, she worked more with his brother in Emergency than with him but was actually in pediatrics. Which would violate his rule about causing stress in the work environment. Stress often led to scandal. It was one of his guiding lights to bring as little extra drama to the floor as possible; these kids and their families went through enough without dealing with that kind of selfishness.

"Okay, but I should warn you I have an early bedtime tonight," Wolfe announced, at least giving himself a plausible reason to leave early. "I can go for the start at least. What time?"

Angel took too long to answer, especially given the way she avoided looking at him, but when she did there were strings of hesitation in the melody of her voice. "Starts at seven. We'll need to get a cab soon to make it."

He could smooth this over. Just be extra friendly to banish whatever doubts she harbored.

"Do I have time to change?"

"If you go now." Angel gave a location to meet and then set about instructing Jenna on how to view the video feed.

Nothing else to do, he directed—just so his trip there wasn't a total loss, "Eat the food, darlin'. We keep our promises, right?"

"I will."

He winked at Jenna, then headed out.

This would be all right; it wasn't a date. The heavenly smelling Dr. Angel was practically mute under most circumstances, even if she was currently trying to melt his Grinchy heart with acts of unexpected kindness with his young patient. She'd revert once they were alone, he was sure of it. Silent and introverted would counterbalance the distracting nature of her scent.

Outside the juxtaposition with the hospital's natural scent, he might not notice her at all.

CHAPTER TWO

HAVING CHANGED INTO street clothes, Wolfe stuffed his hands into his favorite lambskin gloves, protecting them from the already bitter winds of late autumn while he waited for Dr. Conley.

One of the few things in his life that he cared about—the state of his hands. It directly correlated with his ability to do his job to the highest level, which was the one thing that gave him any nobility. The same basic root as the reason he was about to participate in the evening's looming horror show: to be a good doctor for his young patient.

People tended to look sideways at anyone who disliked Christmas as much as he did, and in no way did he ever want to explain his reasons. There really was no way to sufficiently explain without the gory details he'd fled Scotland to remove from his life by removing his parents. Which made this the time for expert-level faking, and he'd found it useful to focus his disdain on whatever subject of Christmas-centered conversation that came up, not the holiday. Trees, for instance. Or caroling. People couldn't balk at him loathing eggnog. He refused to believe people actually liked that slimy abomination anyway. Dressing in ugly jumpers, singing songs that were either far too somber or far too cheerful? Who liked that?

He'd survived a lifetime of this particular yearly sacrifice to materialism, he could do it again. Wouldn't be the last time his acting skills would be called upon this season.

"Hey." Dr. Conley's voice came from behind him, cutting through his rapidly spiraling pep talk, and he turned in time to see her swing on a boxy black coat with oversize buttons. The motion caused the waistband of her red jumper to ruck up, exposing what was either a tiny waist, or the curve of shapely hips. Or both.

The cold winds that had been chapping his cheeks suddenly caressed like a cool breeze on his heated skin and, despite that heat, a shiver ran through him. A flash of socially acceptable midriff and suddenly he couldn't think of a single thing to say.

What was wrong with him? She wasn't *that* attractive.

Sure, she had those fantastic dark blue eyes, and what man wouldn't want to shove his hands into that shining black hair? But it was probably the freckles that were messing him up. He loved freckles almost as much as he hated Christmas.

"You ready?" she asked, apparently not noticing he'd gone stupid, or prompting him because she had. "Can you get the cab? They ignore me."

The request was enough to get him functioning and he did so while silently reminding himself why Conley was off-limits. *Because we don't bring scandal into the workplace. We don't do scandal period.* Scandal never did anyone any good and bringing it around the kids was completely out of bounds. Besides, she was so quiet and serious, he could almost see flashing above her head in neon: *Commitment. Commitment. Commitment.* Not a woman to have a casual, limited-time-only fling—his only type of relationship.

New plan for the evening: be his most ridiculous. Conley never laughed; she'd hate him being anything but seriously festive and seriously serious. Which would keep him from making any hormone-driven mistakes on the off-chance she felt the same pull of sugar-frosted temptation. Besides, Jenna would laugh at him being a dork. Two birds, one big stupid stone.

Once in the cab, he settled in beside her and tried to focus on the unpleasant cab odors rather than the sweet scent she seemed to emanate.

She sat less than a foot away, and the way she snugged the coat around herself and looked the other direction should've made him feel more relaxed about the likelihood she'd encourage him to do something stupid.

The silence sat so heavily even the cabbie was put off by it. Wolfe was usually good at meaningless chatting. Putting her at ease would at least make it easier to get through the evening.

"So," he started, looking back over to find her fidgeting with one of the oversize buttons, tugging and rolling back and forth. "What's the plan? Film the whole thing?"

She stopped flipping the button about and just rubbed at it like a worry stone. "I don't really know. When I offered, it sounded very straightforward. She's going to tell us what she wants to see, and I think she'll see the performances on television. I really don't know what there will be to look at on the ground, but that's what she focused on, that the broadcast was far away, and she couldn't look up at the tree towering above. Probably just the tree. I hope just the tree. Not sure I'll be able to find anything but the tree and the rink."

Although she said a whole lot, she didn't once look at him. She looked everywhere else—out of his window, through the partition to the front seat at the posted license, at her buttons…

Knowing how little she really wanted to interact with him should've made him happy. Really shouldn't have felt like a challenge.

"Start at the tree, then?"

She nodded, fumbling her phone from her pocket and wordlessly typing into a search engine.

"What are you looking for?"

"They get the tree from a different part of the country and a different breed of pine every year." She paused, finally looking over at him. "What?"

"I didn't say anything."

"You're watching me like I'm doing something dumb."

"I'm watching you like you're about to waste time looking for information I already possess." He plucked the phone from her hands, flipped to the camera, took a smirking selfie and handed it back to her.

Her stunned expression made him want to misbehave a little more. With his best rendition of her Southern accent he mimed back, "What? You're watching me like I'm about to do something dumb."

It took her a moment, but her reaction finally caught up with her and the plush mouth that had been hanging open stretched in a slow, bemused smile. "I will…treasure? This?"

There was a question at the end of every word she paused her way through. Then she laughed. An actual laugh that accompanied her turning the phone off and stashing it again.

And just like that, his plan not to get too friendly went up in flames.

"Consider it an early Christmas gift," he murmured. "And the only gift I'm giving this year, so be honored."

"You don't do Christmas with your brother?"

Of course she'd ask about Lyons. She worked with his brother more than she worked with him, but his mention brought up that mixed bag of emotions he'd been struggling to deal with for a while. Before Lyons had been shot, they'd both been content ignoring the holiday, but this year Wolfe just didn't know what to do with his brother. They weren't close, but since last Christmas, Wolfe had been ineffectively trying to change that, and knew beyond any doubt that Lyons shouldn't be alone when *this* Christmas rolled around. But he didn't know how to talk about it. Just as he'd failed to know how to talk to Jenna.

"Lyons doesn't do Christmas either," he said after a lengthy pause.

"Is it a Scottish thing?"

She was funny. Or dumb. Both of which appealed in entirely different ways. "Scotland's a Christian country..."

"Yes, but don't you do gifts on Boxing Day? I'm not entirely sure what that is, to be honest. But there's also the chance that you all do something with kilts and flinging massive logs," she offered, and, instead of turning the phone back on, gave the buttons a rest to flip the case open and closed, open and closed, open and closed.

"The only massive logs I like to fling are the ones that fit into my fireplace." He was supposed to be the one being a dork tonight, but she was getting in the good zings. "How do they celebrate Christmas where you're from?"

Such a simple question, he didn't expect the

color to drain from her cheeks, which only dark-ened the swath of freckles that were thickest at the apples and across her nose.

He knew enough about paling to know that it didn't come lightly and guessed, "That is the face of someone who dislikes Christmas."

"No, it's not," she argued, not a drop of passion in her voice. "I want to see the tree very much. I was going to go anyway. I just wasn't going to stream it."

"Why? It's technically a different tree every year, but it's the same as last year."

"I didn't see it last year."

"Why not?"

"Because I arrived in January," she answered after the slightest pause. With other topics, she spoke easily enough, but when it came to talk-ing about herself? She paused long enough to draw attention to it, like the beat people took to come up with a story before telling a lie. Like every conversation with his parents, which no doubt colored his thinking. Why would she lie about that? Silly.

"For point of reference," she explained, "Jenna was my first patient at Sutcliffe, and I diagnosed the initial mass on her kidney."

And the truth, he was sure of it. Her careful choosing of words was for some other reason.

And he'd performed that first surgery to remove part of the one kidney, which had seemed to come out clean. Which the chemotherapy and radiation should have finished off. It hadn't been a date that had been burned into his memory at the time, but with her relapse and second surgery, he'd become more familiar with it—January 17.

And it explained her connection to Jenna. Why she continued to visit her despite no longer being her physician. He didn't know much about her, except that she was moving to Atlanta and that she needed to be friendlier at work, but being captive in the back of a cab gave him a moment and freedom to ask questions.

"Why are you leaving so soon? Not getting on with someone?"

Again, the small amount of color she'd regained drained away, except for her ears. Her ears went bright, fiery red. Man, he was on a roll with her.

"I just want to go now. But it'll be nice to have some proper New York Christmas activities before I go."

"To Atlanta," he clarified. "I heard you were moving to Atlanta. Want to be closer to family?"

"Look." She gestured out of the window and he followed the motion as the cab slowed.

They'd arrived at the cross street between towering buildings, the plaza a block in. The tree still sat unlit. "We made it in time, I see."

"Thought the crowd and traffic would be worse." She went with the subject change.

He fished cash from his wallet, despite her objection, and paid the cabbie. When he opened the door to get out, the sound of the busy city streets wiped away that strange sense of intimacy he'd been feeling, exchanging it for Christmas music from a jazz band on the corner of 49th and Rockefeller Plaza, doing their best to assure everyone that it was "the most wonderful time of the year."

He didn't buy it.

Angel climbed out of the back seat, trying to shrug off the little squabble that had gone down over who was going to pay the cabbie. It was a kind offer, she knew that. He was being gentlemanly. But all she really felt was an insinuation that she couldn't afford to pay, just like all those times when she hadn't been able to.

When she'd been in medical school, she'd really thought that once she'd begun making a very comfortable living, that fear, that feeling of inadequacy would fade away like so many bad memories.

And she'd run with the notion. She'd been in medical school, hundreds of miles from Knott County, Kentucky, and the local Conley stigma. It should've been safe to be open and share her past—the poverty, the criminal family, the unfortunate time she'd spent in juvenile detention—with the boyfriend she'd thought to love but had lost instead. That mistake had followed her to New York, taking her first job too after she'd had the misfortune to work for a man who knew Spencer, and noticed they shared the same medical school.

Thinking she could get past that here? Wishful thinking. That inadequacy stayed pinned to her, like an errant shadow she couldn't shake off. Sometimes, after the fact, she could rationalize her way through why her first instinctive reactions to the things said to her were wrongheaded, but reason and emotion were different things. She'd been judged too harshly for too long, and, no matter how far she'd run, it had chased her. She expected it now. Sometimes she even thought she deserved it.

Knowing how unlikely it was that McKeag

would think she couldn't pay didn't make it feel any less real, any less pointed. But making a scene over a cab fare would just draw a big circle around her insecurities.

So, she put up the mildest fuss, then moved on.

His small, kind contribution wasn't the same as charity. She didn't rely on charity for anything anymore.

Phone in hand, she stopped on the sidewalk and tried to flip through to the camera and juggle that with the social media account she was supposed to stream through. Not that she'd ever streamed before. But the words had come out of her mouth regardless. Everyone streamed, right? She'd looked up the instructions in the locker room while changing, but now could absolutely not remember the steps.

"Are you waiting for someone else to join us?" McKeag asked. Jenna might call them both by their first names, far too personal for her; he'd be McKeag. Wolfe sounded too…something. Primal.

"No, I'm just—" Just not wanting to admit she was having issues. She could figure it out. She didn't need the help of the walking embodiment of gloriously scruffy, dimpled manliness.

She tapped the icon that was supposed to initi-
ate this nonsense again. Then twice more.

Nothing happened.

"Technological difficulties, please stand by,"
he said, his voice like a surprisingly soothing
narrator, but that damnable brogue played up.

"It's not difficulties. I know how to do it. I
read—"

"Never done it before?" he cut in.

She puffed, didn't answer and mashed the icon
again.

Then he was at her shoulder staring at the little
screen; the firm plane of his chest against her
back and the proximity of his head to hers made
her fumble, nearly dropping the phone.

"Here." He pulled off remarkably nice gloves,
stashed them in his pocket, then wrapped one
warm, firm hand around the wrist of her phone-
holding hand. The heat of his touch spread up
her arm and directly into her chest, making her
muscles go soft and far too pliant. With no effort, he bent her arm slightly, to see the screen.

When he lifted his other arm to reach over
her, which would practically be an embrace, the
bitey critters returned with ravenous delight,
and before she started to squirm against him, or
throw herself shamefully on the pavement with

her butt in the air like Meemaw's ever-horny cat, she turned and pressed the phone into his hands.

He was going to do it, but, God help her, he couldn't put his arms around her like that. The danger of making a complete fool of herself had already escalated when Jenna had tricked him into coming, and, given the choice, she'd rather be judged culturally stupid than accidentally throw herself at him.

She'd just been too lonely for too long. Another reason to move on. Although they were both massive cities, Atlanta and New York City might as well be different countries. Here she tried to speak the language and always sounded wrong, off…dumb. At least there, she'd have the native tongue, even if she had to keep her low-class dialect under control still.

Angel couldn't say she'd had a crush on McKeag the entire eleven months she'd been at Sutcliffe. Those lame feelings had probably taken a good two weeks to colonize and really infect her, leaving her flustered simply by the man's presence, and the chills he could send racing to little-used parts of her body even without all the physical touching. "You do it."

He looked at her for a long second, his blue eyes pale in the center with deep indigo rings around them, giving them a mesmerizing quality under the best conditions. But when he grabbed eye contact like that, and held it, he had to see those frustrating feelings swimming around in her own eyes. It was just *right there*, and it didn't take someone who'd survived childhood by reading other people's intentions to see it.

His eyes were probably the heart of his damnable attractiveness. It wasn't that the rest of him wasn't wickedly handsome—the man had a jaw so square it screamed masculinity, and that mouth. If he didn't stop smiling...heaven help her. She could imagine Lyons laughing about it tomorrow, even if she'd never actually seen him smile.

Just as she felt her heartbeat hit the high millions per second, he broke his gaze away to fix on her phone, not mentioning her lapse into starry-eyed staring. A few taps and he announced, "We're a couple of minutes early. She might not be watching yet, but you know anyone following you will be able to see this, right?"

"Well, sure." She knew that. She wasn't dumb. At least, not all the time. She just didn't know how to start the danged thing. And she really hoped no one else at the hospital would be watching. Being around Wolfe was hard enough.

"If someone starts watching, they're going to be bored pretty quick and turn it off. It's for Jenna, so we're basically just going to walk around and look at stuff."

"Then why were you looking up facts for the tree?" He kept the phone on her, clearly recording, which was not how she'd planned this going. She was going to hold the camera, not have her graceless, stuttering inadequacies immortalized online. "I was just going to tell her what it was and let her know she can look up where the tree came from to see the farm and stuff. I don't know. I didn't really have time to come up with a good plan."

She snapped her fingers for him to hand the thing back over to her and *stop* recording her.

"So, you're not going to play tour guide," he reiterated, still recording.

"No."

He watched her a moment longer, which was at least ten times longer than she wanted him to look at her, then handed the phone back. "Good thing I'm here. The poor kid needs some entertainment."

She looked at the screen and saw four viewers watching, as well as a comment pop up from

Jenna. "She's here. She wants us to go to the tree."

Soon, she expected, the other three watching would drift off somewhere more entertaining. Any second now.

He gestured for her to follow. "Get me in screen. You're just awful at being a cameraman, love."

That was teasing. It sounded like teasing. Not real criticism.

He put his gloves back on and gestured again for her to follow him into the plaza. Was she supposed to film him walking?

While not paying attention to his backside. Oh, Jeez, Jenna did not need a long screengrab of that man's behind while he walked. This needed to be PG, even if her mind had sunk to the depths of at least PG-13 at that precise moment.

Jerking the screen up and *off* him, she panned it over the crowd and toward the tree as they walked. Let Jenna get a feel of what it was like to walk into the plaza. That was the experience. Not McKeag's butt.

He glanced back at her, then, seeing that she was not filming him, fell back until he was in step with her. "You're quiet."

"I'm in awe of the majesty of—" *your behind* "—the crowd." She sighed. "I'm trying to keep it level and not be all super shaky."

"No stabilizer?"

"I have no idea. It's a new phone. It should do all the things."

To his credit, he didn't laugh at her ineptitude. His smile was potent enough, especially when his hand moved to the small of her back and steered her to the left around some people she would've totally seen before running into while futzing with the phone. "She says the cookie place is on the far side of the plaza."

"If it takes cookies, I'll buy a dozen."

If someone could shout an exclamation point with their eyes, Angel attempted it—eyes so wide they might pop clean out of the socket. She jabbed him in the arm with her elbow, so he didn't miss it, and shook her head. Finger over the microphone, she whispered, "Kids take that kind of thing literally. You can't say you'll buy a dozen, she'll expect a dozen and she needs some actual nutrition, not just empty calories."

His adulting skills were also lacking in the child-bribing department. Which somehow made him more attractive.

"Yes, ma'am." He all but saluted, then turned

the camera to him, discreetly moving her fingertip off the microphone. "Lass, you know you can't eat a dozen cookies and nothing else, right? I'm just prone to extravagance, my mum used to say. But I think your mum would whack me with the IV pole if I tried to give you a dozen cookies. So, it's two. Any others that may come back to the hospital must be shared."

She crossed her eyes and shook her head. "There is a two-cookie limit on what will be allowed onto the floor. If you bring a box, all the children—even the ones who can't eat right now—are going to want a cookie and we haven't cleared that with Dietary. This has to be a secret. Secret cookies come in small numbers."

She puffed, then realized it probably sounded like hurricane force winds with her face so close to the camera and switched to reading comments again.

The administrator was watching.

Crap.

"Um, we're…yes, ordered to only bring two."

Back to their tree quest.

He led through the crowd, and she tried to pretend that the gentle steering wasn't nice. It was kind of chauvinistic, really. That was exactly what she'd think if she saw some other woman being led around like that, but somehow he made it feel comforting. Probably nothing to do with *him*; it was a side effect of the ball of nerves in her chest every time she ventured into a proper New York crowd. That many people, packed so close? It was just plain scary. Riding the subway had made her break out in a cold sweat the first couple of times she'd tried it.

The presence of anyone she knew would've felt comforting. Safe. It wasn't anything to do with him.

When they reached the denser crowds, he took her hand instead and cut through the sea of bodies until they were in the crush, three bodies back from the railing that kept the tree safe from the public. That was worse. Even with his fancy gloves, her hand in his wiped all thoughts from her head. All she could do was catalog sensations. All the tingling. The parts of her that trembled and heated. Insanity.

"Look up." His voice was in her ear. She tilted her head back to look up at the tree, and he steered her arm, tilting the camera back.

They'd arrived just in time. The MC began to speak, and she missed every single word the man said. All she could do was stare up at the tree, focus on keeping it steady and try really hard to ignore the feel of him behind her. The crowds of New York were something she could never hope to get used to; they literally pressed so tightly together that the crowd seemed to move like one organism—which meant everyone directly beside her was touching her. So why was it that she only really felt *him* at her back? His heat. His solidity. The fan of his breath on her neck…

Someone flipped a switch and the tree blazed to life, thousands of lights instantly glowing.

It towered over the plaza and glittered as if covered by the wealth of the Rockefeller family. As if someone had opened some vault of jewels and strung the sparkling strands from bough to bough, spiraling upward to a crystal star that wiped out pretty much every thought she'd had before coming down.

So far gone from the strands of threadbare tinsel of her childhood trees. No hulking fire hazards of multicolored lights. No icicles dripping from everywhere because icicles were cheap and covered a multitude of tree imperfections. Icicles, it was well known, could kill your pets while making your Christmas tree seem full and high class. Not true, at least on one count. She hoped not many people lost pets to icicles.

No icicles here, not as she'd known them—though there did seem to be some crystal, icicle-like ornaments among the perfect, colored glass balls.

Did her family still celebrate the holidays? Maybe they'd only ever tried for her. It had been the one time of year she could count on receiving a gift, and only learned as a teenager that most of those gifts had been stolen. For her. For them. She didn't know anymore.

"Ready?" he asked, breaking through the cold fog that rolled over her any time she thought about her estranged family.

"For what?" She looked over her shoulder, but he was already sliding between her and the next nearest body, so he stood more to the front and she could get part of him in frame with the tree.

"This is a stately Northern Porcupine Cone Tree. It was brought to this country approximately three hundred years ago by immigrants from the land of…"

Porcupine Cone? Was that a tree? No way. Three hundred years?

She felt her brows coming down even before he smiled extra bright at her.

He did *not* have the information.

"I don't remember where they came from, but

it was very far away." He gestured up and down, denoting the height, and she finally caught on that he'd changed his accent. He now sounded like a remarkably proper BBC documentary narrator. "This magnificent beast of a Christmas tree is approximately seven hundred feet tall. The Rockefeller family employs twelve brigades of elves—one for each of the days of Christmas—both to make the lights and ornaments and put them onto the tree in the dead of night when the rest of the world is sleeping."

She should stop this, shouldn't she? Her smile said she wanted to hear more of this silliness, but he was lying to the kids and they would believe him. Well, *might* believe him.

But it was kind of amusing? To her, at least.

"Unfortunately, this year there was a terrible scandal in the Elf Union as Old Man Winter outsourced the production of the ornaments to South Pole elves, paying them significantly lower wages than the North Pole Union allows. And thus began the much misunderstood War on Christmas."

CHAPTER THREE

THE REMAINDER OF the ceremony continued in much the same manner—Wolfe narrating in the most outlandish and ridiculous fashion, which made the comments on the stream go berserk, and more and more people tune in to what was supposed to be a temporary, barely viewed feed on Angel's account.

Now she couldn't erase it. Now, although she barely used the thing, each view pressed on her like the weight of a stare. Increased traffic could only lead to increased scrutiny. Increased exposure and danger.

"You might've become an internet celebrity, in my small circle of friends and followers," she murmured as she eyed the three-digit number of people following their—well, *his*—antics.

"Ah, fame. Such a burden. Next thing you know, women will be throwing themselves at me." The ceremony had ended a few minutes ago, but he was obviously still on.

She flipped the phone case shut and walked with him back out of the plaza, because walking was the only way in which she *could* keep up with the man. It was both satisfying and horrifying to know how quick-witted he was. Satisfying because he was a surgeon, he took care of children in extremely critical situations, so him being bright was a good thing, but horrifying because she was a doctor too, she should be able to be as effortlessly witty as he was. Instead, she couldn't work the phone, and she couldn't come up with anything outlandish to say about the tree or the holiday.

"Dr. McKeag…"

"Angel, please, call me Wolfe. We're friends now, right? Or at least we're peers who aren't mortal enemies. Call me Wolfe. I'd hate to think that you didn't enjoy the evening half as much as I did, and I truly didn't expect to enjoy it so much."

Call him Wolfe, as if that made any of this easier. It was a step out onto a rickety bridge over rushing flood waters.

He paused at 49th, where they'd exited the cab earlier, and looked at her, the cookies in one hand and the caddy of hot drinks in the other. "You turned the phone off, right?"

She showed him the closed case, then dropped it into her coat pocket. "Listen, Mr. Alberts was on the feed, so it did go further than I'd hoped."

"Was he?" He handed her the cookies to free his hand to hail a cab, leaving her begrudgingly grateful for his remembering, and saving her asking.

"He was." She tucked the small bag of snickerdoodles into her other pocket and cleared her throat. "And about one hundred and thirty-several people I barely know."

He deserved to know the number, even if it was unlikely to trip him up the way it did her.

"You sound worried."

How much should she admit to? It was unlikely this would snowball into Spencer coming out of the woodwork again to warn Alberts this time. She wasn't even social media friends with him, or anyone else from her epic three-day job, but putting herself out there at all felt like running into a bear's den.

"No, lass," he said, probably because she took so long to answer, slipping into an even more familiar way to address her, a way he usually reserved for patients. Until a rascally light sparked in his eyes, and he followed up with, "I don't feel slightly guilty for this evening. If you feel guilty,

I'm going to have to assume you've been having untoward thoughts about me and all the things you'd like to do to me in the back of this cab."

As he spoke—the velvety rumble of his voice, the way he leaned ever so slightly closer—her cheeks flamed brighter and brighter, and there went her ability to think again.

A taxi pulled up to the curb beside her, but still not a single danged word popped into her head. At least, nothing above a second-grade denial. *Nuh-uh!*

He took her scarlet silence with a grin, opened the door and gestured for her. "I'll let you do the delivering to the hospital without me. I don't think my manly virtue could be sustained if I climbed into this darkened leather interior with you now, Dr. Angel."

He was teasing. She knew he was teasing. Sort of. Probably. She still couldn't think of anything to say back to him, just climbed into the seat and held out her hands for the drinks.

When he'd placed the warm cardboard carrier in her hands, she found her tongue, or at least some semblance of the grace she wished she could display under pressure, and said, "Thank you for accompanying me this evening, Wolfe." Oops. Said his name, and it took a couple of stumbling stutters to finish. "I... I... I'm sure the stream was more interesting to Jenna—and everyone else—because you were narrating it. It no doubt brightened her evening far more than it would've had she not sort of tricked you into coming with me."

He kept hold of the door with one hand and leaned down to speak through it. "I could've found a way out of it, you know. I did give myself an out—early bedtime—should I be having no fun at all. But I was. You're a much better cameraman than you give yourself credit for, Angel."

Before she could say anything else, he ducked in, kissed her cheek in a vigorously platonic but sweet way, which still made her body turn into a human sparkler, and closed the door.

"Which hospital, Dr. Angel?" the driver asked from the front, having heard every word along with her complete inability to keep up with the dashing Scotsman.

"Sutcliffe," she answered, then settled back, balancing the drink caddy between her knees and pulling the phone out again to check the views.

Could people keep watching the video now that it wasn't live anymore?

When she opened the case, all the color she'd built up from Wolfe's teasing drained right away. Closing it hadn't shut it off. It always shut it off. Always. Always, always, always. But not today.

Jenna was still listening, and she'd filled up the comments with several lines of kiss marks and hearts.

If she'd just fallen off the Empire State Building, it still wouldn't have been further or faster than the plummeting in her middle. Thank goodness she'd not had time to eat before the outing, nothing to throw up.

She didn't look at the video, or the state of it, just manually turned the blasted thing off and closed the case again. Just pretend those hearts were Jenna's way of showing appreciation for an entertaining evening. That's all. She was blowing kisses of gratitude and affection.

Not Jenna's way of commenting that she, and countless others, had heard Wolfe's suggestion Angel was about to maul him in the back seat of a taxi.

By the time she arrived at the hospital, Angel had miraculously accepted Wolfe's teasing, but although she wanted to think of it as flirting, the more likely reason was that he was bored, and he'd noticed she was tongue-tied around him.

And the unconcealable starry eyes she tended to have. Her ability to crush in a secretive manner had never really progressed beyond the age where you automatically hated the person you liked the most. So, around ten. She was a ten-year-old trapped in the body of a grown woman, and how ridiculous was that?

The sooner she got to Atlanta, the better. This place was hell on her self-esteem *and* her nerves. That was the problem. She worried about fitting in, then worried about being found lacking, then about the looming threat of public humiliation she'd spent a lifetime trying to outrun. It would come if she stayed. Just a matter of time. Catastrophe. Could still happen in Atlanta, at least if she got dumb again and overshared with someone, but that was something she could control. Here? Nope.

She stepped off the elevator on Jenna's floor and made a beeline to her room. It was late enough that the kid should be sleeping, not waiting up for treats, but at least she could find out whether dinner had happened, and that would ease one worry standing between her and sleeping tonight.

She knocked on the right door and a moment later, before she could even reach for the knob, it swung open and Mrs. Lindsey, eyes glittering and smile too broad to be anything but alarming, invited her in.

"Dr. Conley! We were hoping you'd arrive soon." She relieved Angel of the cup caddy, making her immediately glad she'd bought four cups instead of one. Mr. Lindsey was also there, as well as little Mattie.

"Did you all just get here from the lighting?" Angel eased the bag of cookies from her pocket. Should've bought more than the two cookies she'd argued for—there was a four-year-old boy there too.

"Did you get the cinnamon sticks?" Jenna asked, holding out her hands eagerly enough that her mother stopped everything to set her up with the drink, then did the same with her littlest playing on the floor in the corner.

"We came as soon as they lit the tree, so we could start decorating," Mrs. Lindsey explained. "If Jenna has to be here for any length of time, we're going to make it nicer."

Angel looked around and noticed a few little touches of Christmas that now graced the simple buttery yellow walls. A tangle of twinkle lights and faux pine boughs wrapped around the television. There was also an old-fashioned Santa embroidered on a small blanket draped over the recliner placed in every room for the loved ones who stayed with the littles. Small touches, but heartfelt. Meaningful.

Suddenly, her nerve-inducing, awkward contribution felt completely worth it. Felt like a gift for her as well.

"That's a lovely idea." Angel watched Mr. Lindsey get a sprig of plastic mistletoe to suspend from an empty little hook on the railing upon which the privacy curtain hung. Then promptly snagged his wife by the hand and kissed her cheek.

"If you hang it there, you get to move it around and then it can be anywhere around the bed for everyone to get kisses." There was a wistful quality to Jenna's smile that suggested a boy on her mind, but it passed quickly. "Snickerdoodles?"

Angel didn't comment on the mistletoe or the kisses—that might remind everyone of Wolfe's teasing and she appreciated the small amount of sanity she'd managed to hold on to this evening. Instead, she jiggled the bag and handed the oversized cookies to Mrs. Lindsey to make necessary decisions about distribution.

"When Jenna told us you and Dr. McKeag were going to film the lighting for her, we had no idea how remarkably silly he was. I'm kind of glad I didn't know that before the surgery, I might've thought him unfit for treating my daughter, but he's both a skilled surgeon and an absolute, charming delight."

And another woman in the world fell victim to the charm of Wolfe McKeag.

Which really should comfort her. If anything, he was used to women being dazzled by his eyes, his mouth, his dark, curling hair, that accent, the butt, which she now couldn't forget, and which was still prompting her to think about his other parts. Parts she'd long ago sworn not to think about.

"He's probably the best surgeon on staff," Angel agreed, because, nope, she was unwilling to admit he was charming. Or a delight. Or whatever Mrs. Lindsey had called him. "I really need to get home. I used up my ability to stay awake past my bedtime during residency. Now I sleep just as often as I can and relish my eight hours."

"Thank you for the treats and the recording,"

Jenna said from around her cookie. "I ate half of my soup—it was okay. This is better."

"Tomorrow you're going to eat more, right?" Angel prompted but smiled just the same. "And don't tell Dr. Wolfe, but I had fun with him there, even if I briefly wanted to strangle you for making him go with me. He was…"

"Funny," Jenna filled in for her, and Angel nodded.

"He was funny."

"And cute," Jenna added.

"I'm glad you think so." Angel deflected that one. She buttoned her coat back up and reached out to squeeze Jenna's hand. "Glad you enjoyed the rare Christmas Porcupine Cone Tree."

They all laughed then.

Just as Angel made it to the door, she heard Jenna call, "You should marry him. Then you won't leave New York and you can stay here to help take care of me."

Angel didn't sigh, but her heart did. There was no way to take those words and not ache. Guilt. Sadness. Worry. All vied for top billing in her chest.

For the hundredth time this evening, words failed her. Jenna's statement was equal parts teasing and the current of fear that permeated the thoughts of all people dealing with terrifying illness, but with the straight-shooting of a child.

"You know…" Angel decided to focus on that part and turned back from the door to face her young former patient "…your doctors are great doctors. I don't do anything to help take care of you anymore. I just show up because you're darling and I love seeing you."

"And you're my angel. I know when my mom brought me to see you last winter, no one else was paying attention to my sick feeling, but you did. You're the reason I got better for a while. I need you to stay here in case I get sicker and people don't believe me."

No beating around the bush this time, and Angel felt it into her core.

She could see how it might've appeared that way to a child, but Angel making her diagnosis had been far from remarkable or miraculous. By the time Angel had seen her, the tumor had begun affecting her spine, and that was a lot easier to catch than the earlier symptoms. It had just been much more obvious when Jenna had got to her.

"Honey, everyone will believe us now," Mrs. Lindsey gently interjected, giving Angel some cover.

"You've got the best team," was all she could think to say. It was true, and Angel wasn't even part of the team, she just kept turning up because she cared, and people in pediatrics knew at least that about her, and that sometimes she was a way to get Jenna to do something she'd refused to do.

It took a few more minutes of comforting words and gentle goodbyes for her to extricate herself.

Tomorrow would be an early day, and she'd find out exactly how many of the people who'd watched the stream had hung around for her failure to disconnect it.

And she'd have to tell Wolfe...

Man, if she had any sense at all, she'd call in sick.

Wolfe woke up in a good mood the next morning, and even his irritation at knowing *why* he'd awakened in such a good mood hadn't been enough to shake him out of what he could only call the *warm fuzzies*.

He'd not been simply being polite when he'd told her how much fun he'd had with her, and he had two big problems with that situation. First, Angel was off-limits, and that all felt like a date. Undoubtedly more so because he'd even stopped trying not to flirt with her, for reasons he couldn't quite understand this morning, past the pleasure of it. Especially when his mouth had run off and he'd teased her at the end just to watch those delightfully freckled cheeks turn even pinker than the chilly night air made them.

Not dating at work was important, not a decision he'd made on a whim. It had been the only decision to make after a lifetime of dating had taught him he was utterly incapable of sustaining a relationship. He liked the start of relationships. Hell, he loved the start. Nothing was serious at the start, it was just chemistry and fun, and sex, and what was not to like about all that? All that was great. The problem was his inability to evolve past it.

None of the McKeags were good at relationships. Not him. Not Lyons—Lyons was even worse at them than he'd been before being shot, and that had been pretty awful already. And their parents...two more dysfunctional people there could never be. He still didn't understand how or why they would want to stay married. He'd lost track of the number of public affairs they'd each carried on by the time he was a teenager, and they still never divorced. Fought.

Hated one another. Temporarily separated. Started and never finished a few divorces before getting back together, but after forty years of marriage, they were still at it. And still cheating, last he'd heard. Neither he nor Lyons were in contact with their parents. He doubted they even knew Lyons had nearly died.

Even after the shooting, he and Lyons still couldn't figure out how to talk to one another, and Wolfe seemed to be the only one interested in trying. Yet even with the failure of the closest relationship, here he was, gleefully opening a fresh can of relationship worms with Angel.

With all that and his own history of dismal relationship failures, he'd finally come to accept that work and the lives he could save in his career would be the legacy he left this world. None of these children were his, but they all felt as if they were, at least in part. And that was how he'd ended up with Angel last night: the little girl who felt as if she were his had asked and he'd been helpless to refuse.

The fact that it was also Christmas, something else that left a bitter taste in his mouth, should've only made the whole thing more unbearable.

But hadn't.

Knowing how flustered Angel became around

him made it impossible not to flirt and tease her. Making her laugh, which seemed to be such an infrequent occurrence in her life, made him feel good in a way he truly wasn't happy about, no matter the lies his current mood was trying to sell him.

"You shoulda come with me last night."

Angel's voice came from behind him, her accent more pronounced and drawn out. He felt himself smile reflexively, but then he remembered he shouldn't be smiling just because she was there and tamped it back down again.

He turned, because that was polite, not because he wanted to see her. Early for her shift, just as he preferred to be, she still had the softness of sleep around those dazzling blue eyes, and not a single crease in her scrubs.

"Jenna appreciated the goodies?"

"She shined like a new penny." She walked closer, and, although she looked put together and ready to start work, she was tired. It wasn't just the sleepy adorable eyes; her accent also gave her away. Southern still, but deeper. Less careful, maybe. Less prone to pauses. Lots of long vowels. And her metaphor? Pure country in the heart of Manhattan.

"That's good to hear. Glad it did her spirit good, and I'd thought she'd hoodwinked you."

She sat on the bench beside his locker, slouched there, actually, comfortable with him now? That would be another benefit to their evening, if she relaxed some at work.

Her hands fisted together in her lap, which argued against comfort.

"But you still come with me."

Came. Her accent *was* different. He'd never heard poor grammar choices from her before.

"I promised," he said slowly, unable to look away from her. Something was wrong. "Did something happen?"

"The phone stayed runnin' when I thunk… thought—" She stopped dead for a second, seeming to catch up with the grammar situation, and sat up straighter. "I thought it had turned off when I shut it, it always shuts off, but it didn't. I'm sorry."

Definitely not from Atlanta. Maybe more rural Georgia? Farther south? Was that even how southern accents worked?

It took several seconds before what she'd actually said sank in. It hadn't turned off.

Damn.

What had he said to her when she was getting

into the cab? Something about his manly virtue, that was all he could remember.

He tossed his things into his locker and closed the door, buying time while he came up with a response. Or even a reaction, figure out how dismayed to be.

"I don't know how many people were still there, but Jenna was."

Oh, man...

"I didn't say anything specific, did I?" So much nonsense came out of his mouth when he got on a roll, he couldn't be sure.

"Just that I was going to take advantage of you in the back of the cab."

"No details? Not saying *how* you'd take advantage?"

She shook her head, but the grim set of her mouth stayed put.

That was better than it could've been, what with the way she inspired his imagination ever since...well, longer than a day. It had just gone hyperactive last night.

"Are you angry?" Worry colored her words, and the hands in her lap twisted tighter. Sitting there. Not getting ready for work.

He must be more tired than he'd thought. She was already ready, hadn't come into the locker room for her own benefit. She'd come there to find *him*. She'd looked for him. Wanted to talk to him.

His attention sharpened, shaking off his sleepiness like a double shot of espresso mixed with a pound of sugar, judging by the sweetness spreading in his chest.

"Nah. Accidents happen."

His mouth had been the fault. He couldn't even blame her for the temptation she'd become. If he was well adjusted without miles of relationship dysfunction behind him, he'd definitely break his rules to spend more time with her.

He heard her take and release a deep, relieved breath. "Good. If you were angry, it'd be a lot harder to ask you to come out with me again."

Was this a date?

"Huh?" The confused sound erupted from him on reflex. She wasn't psychic, hadn't just pulled thoughts from his mind. He must be mixing things up again.

"To the center tonight with me, to go ice skating," she clarified, speaking much slower, and that charming, strong drawl tamed to something more refined.

Maybe not a date. At least not on her end. No flirting, he realized. No smiling. No trying to tempt him into fantasizing about things he was already admittedly fantasizing about. She might as well have asked him to take her to have a suspicious mole removed, and she looked both nervous he'd say no, and entirely bothered to be asking in the first place.

Nothing like the *other* colleague who'd been stalking the locker room to repeatedly ask him out for over a year.

Reynolds was far more...he'd say convincing, but she'd yet to convince him. Even with Angel looking more like the last thing she wanted was to spend time with him.

"Why?"

"Because I'm boring, and you didn't see her," Angel said, the disgruntled request turning so hope-filled it almost burned him. "I can't be that amusing. I don't know how, but it did her so much good. She was so happy when I went in last night. If the other kids could watch too, get the same benefit... I don't know, I just think it'd be good for them."

Not a date. He felt some of the stiffness ease out of his shoulders, but the vague feeling of disappointment settling behind made his decision for him. It would feel like a date with his out-of-control id.

"I don't date within the hospital," he said, trying to frame it in a way that was both truthful, and something she could accept, even if it twisted what he clearly understood to be her intent. He looked her dead in the eye as he said the words, because if he was going to turn her down for bogus interpretation, at least he'd give it to her straight.

She sat back just a little, as if her personal bubble had been invaded by his refusal. Or she'd been offended.

The door to the locker room squeaked from around the bank of lockers, and they both paused, but when no other sound came and he looked back at her, she'd stood, putting three feet between them, her arms folded. Offended or angry, but she stayed, her expression stuck somewhere between angry and pleading.

"She watched us and she forgot about what is happening to her. Sometimes the best gift you can give someone is the ability to forget. Even if just for a little while."

His stomach soured.

She hadn't asked again, and she didn't even stick around to hear his reaction to her words. She gave it to him straight too: she thought less of him now. That realization had him on his feet before she'd made it out of the locker room, wanting to stop her, change her opinion of him. To make a concession. He was a good guy, and now he felt selfish. He felt like a McKeag.

The door squeaked again, and he knew she'd left. Had someone been in there before? He hadn't heard movement...

Not that it mattered. This situation would only get worse if he spent more time with her, even under the flag of helping the kids forget. One evening together and he'd already failed not to flirt. Today he'd woken up smiling.

Stopping this right now was the only thing to do. Even if it meant she thought he was just another Arsehole McKeag.

CHAPTER FOUR

"CONLEY?"

Angel was standing behind the nurses' station in Emergency, studying the open cases that had yet to be assigned, when she heard the familiar sound of her name on a Scotsman's lips. In that split second it took for the sound to go from her ears to her brain, her heart lurched and began to beat fast and hard in her chest.

Wolfe had come to see her. Maybe he'd reconsidered. Maybe she wouldn't have to do this alone.

She found herself smiling as she turned toward the voice, even if she'd only wanted to shake him a couple of hours ago. He was too smart to have misunderstood her, unless he thought she was just too backward and shy to ask him out directly.

That killed her smile.

Two of her coworkers, who rarely said anything not work-related, had asked if they were going to the winter charity ball together. People realized she was sparking on him, enough that she was still fighting a smile like a complete goober because he'd come to see her.

Only, when she turned toward the deep, broguey voice, it was the *other* McKeag. Dr. Lyons McKeag. The McKeag who worked in Emergency. Another animalistic-named McKeag brother. With her luck, they were probably spread all over the western hemisphere, each with a macho, primal name, and annoyingly pretty eyes.

Why had she thought that it would be Wolfe when *Lyons* was the one who actually worked in Emergency? Because she was hopeless. Because despite the way he'd turned her down, she'd still take his help if he came around. For the kids. For Jenna.

"Dr. McKeag," she greeted, the urge to smile withering like the last autumn leaf. Lyons McKeag had not gotten the charm gene—he had so little charm that Angel probably had more friends than he did, and she had no friends. But she, at least, didn't seem to be hated. Lyons? Pretty vigorously disliked far and wide. "Is there something I can do for you?"

If this was about the tree-lighting...

"There's a woman in Eighteen with her toddler, and I can't understand a word she's saying." Wolfe's nearly black hair looked better with the startlingly pale eyes, Lyons's was closer to caramel—brown with hints of red undertones. Probably nice to other women. "I'm not even sure if she wants treatment for herself or for the boy. You go talk to her."

He wanted her to translate? She with a twang she couldn't get rid of, and had only managed to cultivate to something a notch above her accent through years of study and effort?

"Why me?" she asked, but did reach for her jacket and shrugged it on, ready to follow him. There was a toddler involved, possibly, and that was reason enough.

"Because she sounds like she just fell off a mountaintop in Tennessee. Like you, only worse."

She flinched, never able to fully control those reactions, and never able to erase them afterward, no matter how hard she tried.

Fell off a mountaintop was exactly the shade of her natural speech patterns that she tried to remove, first by identifying and killing the colloquialisms that had once peppered her speech, and still sprang up on occasion, then by addressing the mispronunciations and questionable grammar of her coal country roots.

No one at Sutcliffe, aside from maybe someone in Human Resources, knew where she was from. People assumed Georgia—as Wolfe had when bringing up Atlanta—and she usually let them. Georgia was high-class southern. Even among the rural poor, being considered a Kentucky hillbilly held stigma.

Here in Manhattan? Spencer's reaction and interference had made it clear: she might as well go shoeless and make moonshine on her fire escape for as distasteful as people would consider her because of the unfortunate geographical circumstances of her birth. And that was without knowing her family were the most notorious thieves—and worse—in Knott County. And really without knowing about her own short-term incarceration. No one believed it when someone said they'd been convicted despite being innocent; they'd *laugh* if she admitted she was convicted because of her own lying confession.

In that context, Tennessee was a leg up. Even if it was still handed to her in the form of dismissal.

"You tell me what she's saying," he ordered. "I'll work out how to treat her."

Translator. That was all he wanted her for? Was this another slam on her sounding just as if she fell off a mountain in Tennessee? Felt an awful lot like a slight to her intelligence and capabilities.

"No." The word erupted from her on pure reaction. Seemed to be happening a lot lately, and she could only hope it was because of exhaustion and knowing she wouldn't be here long enough to reap the consequences of fighting back.

Being agreeable was part of the persona she'd carefully constructed, but the idea of him speaking to whoever was in Room Eighteen with the same dismissal? No.

"I'll see the woman and her child in Eighteen. You go find another patient."

Somewhere in all that, she'd stopped walking and now he stopped too. The elder McKeag, the one who growled at everyone all the time anyway, looked at her with such shock it compelled her to restate her objection without the pointed tone she knew had crept in.

Be civilized.

"Dr. McKeag, if it is the mother who requires treatment, I can still treat her. Children are my specialty, but when they grow up, they are still of the same species with the same basic troubles." Okay, not as civilized as she'd been aiming for. Maybe she shouldn't be hoping for Wolfe to visit with her; she already seemed to be picking up his bad habits—sarcasm being right at the top of the list. "If it's somehow outside the bounds of my knowledge, I'll come *find* you."

The long *i* of her *find* annoyed her. That was something she might never conquer, the long *i* that refused to go away no matter how many elocution lessons she took.

He fixed her in an uncomfortable stare for several long seconds, making darned sure she knew he didn't like her—not that she thought he liked anyone—then Lyons McKeag waved her ahead and stormed back the way they'd come.

A minute later, she introduced herself to Becky Davis and asked what was wrong.

"I think he got poisoned." Becky's words came whispered, as if giving them full voice would make the poison instantly kill her son. She shifted the pink-cheeked toddler on her lap as he dozed against her chest, in no distress Angel could see. Not the sort that would indicate poison.

She reached over and brushed back the curly blond hair stuck to his forehead, sweat evincing a fever even before Angel's touch to his face confirmed it.

She grabbed the thermometer from her pocket and placed it against his forehead for a reading.

"Did he get into cleaning supplies under the sink or something? Why do you think he's been poisoned? What symptoms does he have besides fever?" she asked, taking her stethoscope from around her neck so she could listen to him breathe while his obviously distressed mama explained.

"We got in them toxic gases from the sewers. Then he took to coughin' terrible."

Another moment listening, and she confirmed that his lungs did sound wet, and musical in a way that suggested bronchitis. Although Becky's story sounded alarming enough to ask, "You had him in the sewer?"

"No!" Her denial was swift and loud. "We was on the street. Then all these gases come up from the...the..." she waggled her fingers toward the floor "...grates?"

Gases on the street from the grates?

"The steam?" Angel tried to clarify.

Ms. Davis looked at her sleeping and sickly little one and then back to Angel, hope blooming in her eyes. "That was *steam*?"

And then right behind the hope, the certainty that life couldn't work out like that. That Angel was wrong, that the gases were toxic, and that she was just inches away from losing her child. Even Lyons, who was apparently as thick as a coal slurry, couldn't mistake the concern she had for her child. Sure, she also had kind of a thick accent, and maybe she had the same sort of questionable grammar that Angel still worked to rid herself of, but it wasn't like a *real* accent. Her native tongue was still English.

"Where were you when it happened? Was it hot?"

"It was hot, but it just got the edge of us, didn't really burn."

"Yesterday?" She'd heard about one of the city's ancient steam pipes bursting yesterday and the steam coming up through any vent possible until they got the big orange and white stack over it and a crew below the streets to repair the surprisingly eco-friendly Victorian power source Manhattan still used. But the steam was hot and dangerous. It could actually kill, just not through poison.

"Yesterday." She nodded. "We—me and my husband—was walking around with Bobby and it just come up from nowhere, right in front of us. It was hot, but wasn't on us. And then we went back to the place we're staying, and he got sick fast after that and has got worse ever since."

And as a concerned mother, she was both looking for help for her child, and afraid that this place she'd brought him to would hurt him. Mommy guilt knew no cultural barriers.

For the next fifteen minutes, Angel took her time examining Bobby, comforting Ms. Davis and taking a swab that shortly confirmed her diagnosis.

Unfamiliar territory could be scary, and good parents—no matter their education or economic background—worried they weren't doing the best for their children.

Her parents hadn't been like that. None of her family had ever displayed any real sense of kinship, but she'd seen it in the darkest hours in the emergency rooms where she'd worked, and, despite the horror she sometimes encountered there, that was what kept her coming back. It was where she got to see, in the brightest, most authentic and raw terms, what family was supposed to be. What love meant without restrictions and conditions.

New York's cultural diversity, more than any other city where she'd lived, let her see it in people who looked like her, and also in those who looked and believed completely different than she did.

Ms. Davis could've been her neighbor, and Lyons McKeag pushed Angel to her because people still liked to categorize like to like. Which meant two things: that disdain he showed for this woman was really the heart of how he felt about *her*. She was right to keep as much as she could about her background hidden.

And two, Wolfe probably felt the same sort of superiority. Their family was socially important in Scotland, that she knew. And moneyed. Even if he played the fool and charmed everyone, a man couldn't wear handmade gloves and still mix with common riff-raff.

No matter how far she moved, or how far she climbed, she'd still be one of "Those Conleys from Tarpin Holler."

It was nearly 1:00 p.m. before Wolfe's morning surgery was over and he was free to go find Angel.

With any luck, she'd be at lunch, and joining her for lunch in a busy cafeteria was closer to private and unsuspicious than cornering her in Emergency.

In the hours since the locker-room failure, Alberts—the hospital admin—had summoned Wolfe and made clear the *hospital* wanted them to continue, but to watch the flirting. Wolfe had managed not to roll his eyes at that little addendum. Alberts didn't approve of romance at work, something Wolfe generally agreed with— he wasn't some teenager who needed reminding.

He could say no to the request, but he liked his job; it was the best part of who he was. Either the squeaking door had been Alberts overhearing them directly, or someone had reported back to him, maybe even Angel. Now he had to make this work somehow. To come up with some other way to deal with this.

Like throw money at it. He could hire entertainment to come in every evening—that would take the kids' minds off their illnesses while saving him from spending too much alone time with Angel.

He stepped into the still-crowded cafeteria and looked over the bay of tables. Hers stood out for its sheer emptiness.

She'd chosen the smallest table, off by the wall, out of the way. With three empty chairs, she sat, book in one hand, fork in the other, a large salad bowl on the table before her.

Finally, something going his way today. His young patient's surgery had been successful, but more difficult than they'd anticipated, but he shouldn't discount the win. It was just *this* problem and Alberts earlier...

Crossing the cafeteria, he pulled out a chair beside her and sat. The surprised expression she lifted to him was bright and warm for the shortest moment, then visibly cooled before he'd even said a word.

Maybe it was the lack of a greeting earning him the glower. Or maybe she was still angry.

He started over. "Hi."

She laid her paperback down on the table, preserving her location, and set the fork down as well to focus on him. "If you haven't changed your mind, I don't have anything to say to you."

Definitely angry still. Not about to come around easily.

He leaned back in his chair, reconsidering his approach to just lay things out. "What if I have a counter plan to offer?"

Her head turned slightly, those gorgeous dark blue eyes cold, but she was listening. Listening, because she had nothing else to say to him. That shouldn't smart but did.

"You're right that I don't want to let the kids

down," he said. "How about I hire different entertainment to come in every evening, take their minds off the world for a while? Whatever you think would be good."

"You don't want to be involved, so you want to give me money to do stuff for the kids in your name?"

When she put it like that, it sounded pretty jerky. "I wasn't looking for credit."

"But you're feeling guilty over not wanting to invest your time?"

She didn't know about Alberts's order. Which meant it was definitely whoever had been behind the squeaky door that had led to Alberts's intervention.

If he told her that, she'd think even less of him.

God, how did he get himself into these situations?

Screw it. He liked to live his life as open and honest as possible. "Alberts wants us to continue as PR for the hospital."

She pushed the bowl away. "I see. And you don't want to. I get it. I don't need you for some half-hearted investment of your presence. I'll tell Alberts I don't want you there."

Being entirely uninvolved wasn't in the cards.

"You said ice skating. You're planning on going to live stream the rink? That's boring."

"I'll skate and, I don't know, maybe I can strap it to my chest to give that gliding feeling, be kind of at eye level for many of them. Or show my skates on the ice like point of view, they can imagine it being their skates."

"Seriously? That's your best idea?"

She shot him a heated look, picked up her book, marked her place and stuffed it into a satchel on a chair.

"I have time to come up with another idea. There were a lot of people who watched, I don't know how many were from the children's ward, and I know they'll be watching again." Her speech got faster and a little more high-pitched as she spoke...or ranted at him. "I already told Jenna I was going to the rink. It doesn't take much to get the kids excited—anything that breaks the monotony is enough. Even if it's just three or four kids who winds up watchin', I'm not aimin' to disappoint them. I'll figure somethin' out."

Aimin' to disappoint? Figure somethin' out? There was that accent again. Not just a circumstance of being tired. Apparently, it came out when she was angry too.

He could feel a headache starting at the base of his skull. "You won't come up with something better between now and then. I'll come to man the camera. You do the skating."

"Just so you can make snarky comments on how much I stink at skating?" she asked, then paused, clearly considering whether her humiliation was something she'd be willing to offer up.

"You don't know how to skate?"

She picked up her bag, ready to make her escape.

"Okay, no, I never skated before, but I can learn. I do know how to make the danged thang stream this time for darned sure." She swung the bag onto her shoulder, stepped away, then stepped back to jab her finger at him. "You come, or you don't come, I don't care. But if you come, you better come with a glad heart, or not a'tall. I'll be fine without your unkind assistance."

Come with a glad heart? Even with her country twang all riled up, she set a high bar.

It was probably his fault Alberts even wanted them to continue—if he hadn't been messing around, it would've been less entertaining. Messing around and being an idiot to make people smile was an integral part of who he was, but he didn't feel like smiling right now.

Or even feel like making her smile. If it weren't for Angel being involved, he'd be down with the request—for the kids, not Alberts's PR campaign—it was just his *glad heart* got corrupted by his *baser heart*, the one that wondered how far down those freckles traveled over her pale skin. And then everything got complicated and harder to navigate.

"I'll be there at seven," he muttered, then added—because no matter what he wasn't going to make fun of her skating, especially when *she* was the one doing this for the right reasons; he was still the jerk—"I'll film. You come up with something to say. As cute as you are, the kids aren't going to be impressed by your freckles or your ability to impersonate an owl when you have to say something."

"What does that mean?" she asked, loudly enough that people at the nearest tables turned to watch them. Arguing in the cafeteria? If people weren't already talking…

Wolfe mimed the slow blinking she did when stymied by a turn in the conversation. "Some people are naturally quiet, I get it. Introvert, all that. And those people—by which I mean you—aren't really good at conversation. Maybe you should think of some story to tell the kids before you strap your skates on. Or learn some rhyming poem."

She looked for a moment as if she was about to swing that lumpy satchel at his face, but, rather than argue, just turned and walked away.

As one did when they were no good at conversation.

Tonight couldn't end like last night if she was this angry. It was easier to resist the urge to flirt with a woman who clearly thought him a bastard.

CHAPTER FIVE

ANGEL CLIMBED FROM the back of her taxi, her puffy trench coat cinched and buttoned to contain the outfit she'd purchased for the evening's affair, and slung the duffel bag stuffed with the rest of it onto her shoulder.

That was something else she would miss about New York City: the ability to buy almost anything at almost any hour of the day. Her shift at the hospital had ended at three, and from there she'd gone directly to several stores to be certain she was well equipped for the performance she was determined to give.

The taxi pulled away and she looked up and down the street. Was he really coming? Maybe she should wait for him.

No. He might not show up, and she'd be better off waiting at the rink. The closer she was to the ice, the more likely she was to do what she'd intended—skate in this ridiculous outfit—than if she had to stand here where she could easily talk herself out of it and catch a cab home.

Right. Rink it was. She started up the sidewalk toward the rink below the glittering Christmas tree.

"Conley."

Even with her lingering irritation with him, hearing him call her name from behind her shot a little thrill through her belly.

Only ten steps into her journey, she stopped. He'd recognized her with the shiny fuchsia leggings peeking out from beneath a camel-colored trench coat, with her hair piled up in an extremely messy bun on top of her head? From behind? And she'd mistaken *his brother's* voice for his earlier...

She turned around and waited.

How could she have made that mistake? Lyons almost sounded American when he said her name, but Wolfe still laid on the *o* hard enough to sound as if he'd just stepped out of the Highlands. Or not. Given her fixation on losing her own deep Appalachian accent, she suddenly felt kind of bad for not knowing if there was more than one Scottish accent out there. Maybe he didn't sound like the Highlands at all. Maybe

Highlanders didn't sound like what Americans typically thought of as a Scottish accent.

Except for Lyons, who barely sounded Scottish, but had a great deal more judgmental jerk dialect in every word.

Something she'd have to find out online, because, no matter how common this confusion probably was, she didn't like exposing when she lacked in any way. Ever. Especially when she never knew if something was *common knowledge* that she just didn't know.

He caught up to her in seconds, looking so grim a spike of anxiety hit her guts.

"Did something happen to Jenna?"

"What?" He tilted his head a notch, then frowned. "Not that I'm aware of. Why?"

"You look like something is terribly wrong."

"Your legs."

"What's wrong with my legs?" She leaned forward to see them, still there, still brightly colored.

"They're bright pink and sparkly enough to suggest you're about to do something stupid. Humiliate yourself without ever stepping on the ice."

My God, the man's accent. It somehow sounded like a sexy dare when he said *do somethin' stupid*.

She squinted at him, as if that would negate his damnable attractiveness. "I'm not going to do something stupid."

Wait. Yes, she was.

"I'm going to have fun," she corrected. "Like you had fun last night. Even if it takes a humiliating outfit."

All decked out in silliness of the flesh while he'd been decked out in silliness of manner. Which was some semblance of the truth.

He snagged the front of her coat between the gaping buttons and gave a light tug, starting to look begrudgingly amused. "Are you wearing padding?"

Being questioned about her silly outfit when she could still catch a taxi was far from helpful. It also made her cheeks go warm in a way that countered the frosty air.

"Yes, but you can't see the padding."

"I wasn't going to ask for a show and tell, lass, but the trench coat makes your bottom look… let's say…fluffy."

Her bottom *was* fluffy. Because of the tutu. And the miles of cotton batting she'd shoved into the seat of her tights to protect her tailbone. The tutu had been a practical afterthought to hide the fact that the volume of her bottom had nearly tripled and was lumpy enough to resemble some mutant version of super-cellulite.

"And I have kneepads." She didn't bother trying to walk him through the absolute rationality of her safety-first sparkly pink outfit, just pulled her phone out, opened the case and pulled up the post she'd readied on the way over for the stream, and handed it over to him. As soon as she was free of it, she practically jogged to the rink.

He was tall enough to keep up with seemingly no effort, while the increased activity in the cold air made her breathe fast enough to regret having missed so much gym time the past couple of months.

He didn't say anything else until they'd gone through admission and found a spot near the ice for her to get her skates on, which was when she noticed he had a pair too.

"Are you going to skate? I thought you were too cool for ice skating."

"These are rescue skates," he explained, sitting beside her. "I *know* how to skate and plan to be prepared for when I have to come drag you off the ice when you fall and break your arse. Of course, that plan was hatched before I saw your massive arse-padding, but I'm still going to wear them."

She whacked him on the arm on reflex. "You just jinxed me. You know if I fall now, it's all your fault."

Her arm swat made him grin, the jerk.

"I know nothing of the kind. I know that if you fall, it's because of physics. And that you're a rubbish skater."

She grunted, dug her kneepads out and the leg warmers she'd also purchased, and shoved her feet through both before she went about getting the skates on.

"The kneepads don't match."

"They didn't have any pink sparkly ones, or I'd have gotten them." She tied the skates on. "They'll protect as well as the pink ones would've. I hope."

"The imaginary pink sparkly ones? I reckon they would've protected better, being imaginary and all that."

"Shut up." She dug in her bag, got the furry pink earmuffs, crammed them onto her head and topped it all off with the crowning piece of her ensemble. Literally.

The cheap rhinestone tiara had traveled well, despite her rough treatment of the bag, and she wrestled it over the earmuff band, then, before she lost her nerve, unfastened the trench coat, whipped it off and threw it onto the bench.

In her mind, it had all gone very smoothly. In practice, she almost knocked herself down with the jerky ripping around of material, and her tutu remained so mashed up in the back that it didn't at all cover her lumpy rear end until she began frantically smashing and rearranging it.

Wolfe's laughter drew the eyes of everyone else in the immediate vicinity. Not her outfit. They were looking at the loud Scotsman laughing. *That's all.*

"I warned ya I was gonna make it fun." She pointed a pink-gloved finger at him. "Even if you wasn't."

Her words caught up with her mind as soon as they were out of her mouth and did more to wobble her nerves than the outfit did.

"Weren't. Weren't going to make it fun." She corrected herself before he could do it. The more riled up she got, the more upset or angry, the more it came. The twang. The lazy pronunciation. The identity she'd stuffed down far enough one would've thought she'd be able to forget it entirely by now. But there it was, still close enough to the surface to burst forth when she least wanted.

Today Lyons had almost triggered it. He hadn't said the word *stupid*, but it had been there in his open frustration with understanding her, the implication that she'd speak more as he wanted her to speak if she were *smarter*.

Wolfe had a way of tilting his head at things that struck him as curious, and, yes, it conveyed his notice of peculiarities, but it also amplified how awkward she felt about her mistakes, her failings.

"Start the stream." She gestured with one rolling, impatient hand. "It takes a couple minutes for people to start showing up."

All around, people in colorful—and generally warm—outfits slid over the ice. They sat, cueing up a video stream while people who were in no doubt far better moods than the two of them swirled over the ice, festive and bright.

"It's up," he said, standing and offering her a hand up, protectors still on the blades of both their skates. "Do you need instruction, Dr. Angel?"

His question was gentle, almost kind, until he added, "Or did that…majestic skating outfit imbue you with the power of the Ice Capades?"

"Still going to narrate, I see." By the end of the evening, she'd probably be known throughout Sutcliffe as Dr. Puffybutt.

She made a face at him, until he turned the camera on her and she remembered she was supposed to be smiling and happy for this performance. No one liked a grumpy ice skater. "Any tips you have on remaining upright, I'm open to hearing."

There, said without a single dropped *g* or an ounce of her natural twang coming through.

Without any ribbing, he propped the phone up on the duffel bag to record them, took her gloved hand to offer support while he instructed from the ground up. How to remove the blade covers. How to find her balance. How to move. How to fall for least damage, a jinx if she'd ever heard one.

It wasn't much help; theory was a great deal different from application. By the time he'd retrieved the camera and returned to take her hand as she stepped onto the polished glassy surface of the ice, pretty much everything he'd said about staying upright left her mind. Even with them both wearing gloves, it felt like a touch, skin to skin. Distracting. And gallant. And infuriating.

And exactly what she'd asked of him: come with a glad heart. She was the one having trouble with that right now. Not because she didn't want to amuse the kids, but she really didn't like being the center of attention—exactly what her glorious outfit had assured.

Right. Time to make with the glad heart. She let him help her glide the first few feet, then let go.

She hit the ice without even trying to muster her own locomotion. Her feet just went right out from under her and the thick layer of cotton she'd stuffed into her tights didn't make any difference to the volume of the grunt she loosed when she hit, and did nothing to dispel her desire to rub her smarting rear end in public. She resisted. Barely.

Over more than half an hour, Wolfe stood on the side of the rink while she went back and forth in about a ten-foot stretch of ice, trying not to think about how she looked. Really glad she couldn't hear whatever he was saying on the stream about her skating skills.

Had she stayed upright more, there would've probably been ruts worn in the ice, but, lucky for the ice, she polished it enough with her tutu butt to keep that from happening.

Every time she fell, he asked if she was all right. Then asked what she did wrong or gave her some kind of advice that was basically meaningless. At least, until the last fall.

It was almost at exactly an hour when she tried a particularly bold move of trying to stand completely up instead of continuing that kind of half-crouch, knees bent, arms stuck out for balance position she'd been living in.

The crouch kept her center of balance low, and most closely resembled the stance of a toddler just letting go of the table for the first time. And that was pretty successful, all things considered.

She was gliding, gliding, gliding, the slight breeze on her cold cheeks probably just an effect of the weather because she wasn't moving fast enough to create current. As soon as she looked over to Wolfe to show him her I-straightened-my-legs victory smile, she hit a bump. Or maybe she hit nothing at all. Her feet just went opposite directions suddenly, and no amount of rapid scrambling steps could keep her from going down hard on her knees.

It took a couple seconds for the pain to hit, and the realization that her knee pad had drifted off one knee. And it was a lot. The pain was enough to make her gasp and her eyes sting.

The realization she'd done some actual damage didn't arrive until Wolfe was on the ice, his hands under her arms, lifting her up. That was when she saw the red spot on the frosty, bluish-white ice.

Angel grabbed at Wolfe's shoulders, but couldn't put any weight on her leg without wanting to cry.

"Oh, I *benastied* it..." she mumbled, shifting her weight to her left leg, heedless of what it might do to his balance. She couldn't stay upright on her own, so how he could stay upright for both of them was anyone's guess.

"Benastied?" he repeated, drawing her attention to the word she'd selected. God bless it, she had to stop that.

"Hurt." She tried the simpler, less colorful, less colloquial synonym, and didn't even try to explain the word to him. Or why it'd come out. Or anything to draw further attention to it.

"Think you can keep stable on the one foot while I steer us to the side?"

"Cain't promise," she said, and then repeated, *"Can't.* Cannot. Can't promise."

He took the babble for the *no* it was meant to be and, in a feat of extreme showing off, picked her up and skated to the edge of the ice, stepped onto the platform, then set her down on the bench, as if it were nothing. As if he were suddenly Brian Boitano, king of the ice, and she were a dainty little ice dancer instead of the woman who made it to the gym maybe twice a week and probably shouldn't have eaten that ice cream last night.

The red spot saturating her tights was nearing her adorable fuzzy pink leg warmers and she shoved the one down so that it bagged at her ankle. "I don't have anything to blot with…"

He pulled a handkerchief from inside his jacket pocket and pressed it into her hands, then grabbed the material on either side of the seam running down one side her leg and ripped a hole, exposing her bloody knee to the air.

She hissed as much from the material suddenly ripping off the wound as the cold air hitting it directly, and then covered with the hanky. "Did you get a look?"

"There's a pretty nasty gash."

"Was there something sharp…?" She tilted her head to look toward the spot where she'd fallen, but it was just smooth ice with a bit of blood on it.

"No, just an unfortunate landing on something very hard."

"Bashing laceration…" She puffed and tried to straighten her leg, but the heavy skate dragged hard and she whimpered.

He stayed where he was, kneeling at her feet, and unfastened the laces. "Let's get this off."

"I want to go back out." She swallowed, tried again. "Let's just get it to stop bleeding and have a little rest."

"Why on earth would you go back out there?"

"Because you have to stand back up when you fall down. You have to do the things even when they're hard, and you get better at it." And that was when she remembered they'd been filming, streaming to whoever had stayed around long enough to see her fall and get up, over and over again. Where was the phone?

"You really want to get that much better at skating that you're unwilling to stop when you've hurt yourself?" His tone said she was nuts, but she had a purpose. This whole evening had a purpose. Not just to entertain.

"I knew I'd spend the whole night falling down. But I wanted them to see that we get hurt, and get back up. We keep fighting."

Her lower lip quivered and she pulled her gaze away from him, embarrassed by the line of water rising from her lashes to wobble her vision.

"Love, you showed them that repeatedly." His words were gentle, and his bare, ungloved hand touched her chin, guiding her gaze to his. "And now you're showing them that we all need time to recover from hurts. We'll come skating again before Christmas. When your leg is feeling better."

The sincerity and tenderness in his eyes almost made her lose what was left of her emotional control after a long, stressful day. But she believed him. He'd come back with her another day, and they'd do better.

Swallowing, she nodded, and, although she wanted nothing more than to feel his arms around her again in that moment, pulled it together enough to say, "We should comment on the stream. Tell them I'm okay."

He looked from her to where he'd propped the camera up before going to help her. It was still running. She'd gotten distracted in the sweetness of his ministering, and just assumed that, since he wasn't holding the camera, it wasn't running anymore. They weren't in frame, but it was close enough it was likely they were once again overheard.

Reaching for it, she turned a difficult smile to the camera and selfied her first video. "I'm all right. It's got a— Well, it's cut. So, we're probably done for the evening, need to go bandage it."

"Stitch it," Wolfe corrected.

"Stitch it?" she repeated, and then put the phone beside her on the bench to pull up the edge of the formerly white cotton handkerchief. Gash. At least two inches across, and open. Very open. More blood oozed forth and she was forced to cover it again and swallow a couple times to make sure she wasn't about to turn into a big crybaby on the stream.

"Okay, it needs like…four or five stitches. So, we're going to go down to the ER, and maybe Dr. Wolfe will stitch it up for me because he's such a gentleman."

"He will," Wolfe said, and she turned the camera to him. "Goodnight everyone. Stay warm, be good, sweet dreams."

She let that be the closing, purposefully turned the stream off. Double-checked that it was, indeed, no longer streaming, then turned the phone off—all the way off—closed it and stashed it in her duffel.

"So, ideas on bandaging?" she asked.

"Do you think it's broken?"

"I think it's just cut, but every time I put weight on it, feels like the gash up and opens again."

"It's not closed, lass. That's why it's opening up."

"I didn't bring bandages," she said, "because with the safety measures, well, I didn't think I could actually hurt myself that badly."

"Let's get that crooked tiara off your head, and maybe the tutu."

"Not the tutu."

"Why?"

"I have cotton in my pants enough to make my bottom resemble a lumpy hippopotamus."

"Tutu's hiding it?"

She nodded, and he laughed. "Right, well, then let's just get you to the street so we can get a cab, and work on the rest."

Fifteen minutes later, with much of her insane costume removed, material ripped off her legging to tie around her knee, and a strong arm around her waist to make walking easier, they made it to the street and into the back of a cab.

Once they were in motion to Sutcliffe, Wolfe said, "Do you really want to go into work in that tutu?"

He was right. Looking like a fool on video for the *kids* was one thing, but for her peers?

"Not especially," she admitted, but then the whole butt situation made it preferable. "But…"

"Butt," he amended, cutting off her re-explanation. "Lean forward, I'll drag the batting out and stuff it into your duffel."

"You mean you're going to stick your hands down my pants and pull all the cotton out?" she clarified, because the world had just gone insane. And Wolfe was leading the charge, with the bitey things in her belly trembling and starting to chew.

"Or you could take off the tutu and fish it out yourself. It's a little hard to keep pressure on your knee with one hand and dig around in your pants with the other while leaning forward."

Leaning off the cotton was necessary, her leg didn't want to help brace her off the seat, she needed a hand to do the lifting and the other to do the pressure thing. He was right, she'd have an easier time if she just let him stick his hands in the back of her pants.

He was a doctor. Just because he was also a Sexy Scottish Scoundrel didn't mean he wasn't also a doctor.

With a sigh propelled from the depths of her feet, she unfastened the tutu, so it fell away as she leaned up on the other hand, away from him, exposing the fat, lumpy mass she had going on back there.

His soft chuckling as he dipped his hand repeatedly into the back of her tights—knuckles brushing the bare skin and areas where her more sensible cotton panties covered most everything. Still, it was some strange, heady mix of sexy and humiliating to have him pulling wads of cotton from her pants.

"You're done, right?"

He made some noise, then actually patted and prodded her butt and thighs from the outside of her leggings to make sure there was nothing else in there that wasn't *her.* "Done."

She eased back. "I thought so. Everything back there got colder."

"I'm going to resist all the innuendo in my head about how I could warm up everything back there," he said, making her head snap to the side to facilitate her need to stare at him.

Mischief in his eyes, and in that smirk he wore, he continued stuffing the cotton into the duffel she'd carried, along with the tutu.

"Thanks." What was she thanking him for? The word just came out like polite, conversational filler. Thanks for helping. Thanks for resisting the innuendo, that he didn't actually resist? Thanks for putting that mental image in her mind? All options worked. At least she wasn't blinking like an owl at him tonight.

"Look at the bright side—Alberts can't ask us to do anything quite so physical for the rest of these shenanigans. He might not even expect you to continue them."

CHAPTER SIX

THERE WAS NOTHING subtle or sneaky about their trip to the ER. While Wolfe had privileges at the hospital, he had to launch a mini siege on the current ER attending to get to treat Angel himself. It was a catch-22—either he could cause drama at work or just let her go into the queue and wait it out for whatever doctor ended up treating her, a betrayal after the little allegiance they'd forged tonight.

He stepped into the staff room where he'd left her to throw his weight around with the attending, and found her sitting in the wheelchair, ripped leggings, bloody knee peering under the edge of the makeshift bandage.

"You're going to start bleeding again before we get into a treatment room," he said, and she whipped her head up, the guilty expression amid all the pink as cute as her freckled blush.

Allegiance? At that precise second, Wolfe realized the word was too shallow to apply. He *liked* her. He didn't just find her entertaining, or intriguing because she was so bloody strange at times, he genuinely liked her. Images of taking her back to his home, of her reclining in his bed with an ice pack on her knee, made his stomach do an unwelcome little flip.

And he'd thought this evening would be easier on his willpower.

"I don't think it's broken, at least. That's something, right?" she said, completely missing the conflict she had brewing in his mind.

"Have some pink, sparkly X-ray goggles in that duffel bag I missed?"

"Don't need 'em," she said in an I'm-an-ER-doctor-and-I-know-some-junk sort of way.

"We'll see how well you can stand after it's stitched." He grabbed the handles of her wheelchair and pushed her into a small treatment room that remained unused except in times of extreme high volume, like what came with large-scale tragedies, then helped her shift onto the table.

"Did Beetlejuice give you trouble?"

He'd already assembled the supplies he needed before fetching her, and had just gone to the sink to wash up, but her nickname for Dr. Backeljauw, the attending, made him smile. "Why do you call him that?"

"If you say his name three times, he turns up and something bad happens," she murmured. In fact, she'd said his name low too, as if she believed the man could hear her speaking it from anywhere.

"I told him Alberts would be upset if his PR skating star was left bleeding longer than necessary because I'm not on duty and he's having fits."

She groaned. "I think you might get your wish about that, if this is the mess it seems like it might be."

He rolled the stool over with one foot, put his gloves on and retrieved the rolling tray with his other foot before sitting.

"I'd keep a week of ridiculous pageantry if it could save you a busted knee, lass." It was true, no matter how much he wished it weren't. He never wanted to cause pain, but he really didn't want to cause her more than she'd already had—because something told him there was a lot of darkness in her history. She was too sweet to keep herself so far removed from everyone without a good reason.

"I'm going to untie this now, but I'll numb it before I start cleaning."

She scrunched her face up but nodded. "I'm

going to watch you. It's not cause I think you're gonna do a bad job, I just need to see."

"Rather do it yourself?"

"Nope." She answered fast. "Just need to watch. It hurts less if I watch, then I'm not surprised by anything."

"Well, I'll be numbing it good, so that should be the most painful part of this."

"The most painful part *after* removing that hot-pink stretchy bandage, because I can tell ya right now it's sticking."

And that'd mean mechanical debridement if he just ripped the makeshift bandaging off. "I'll hit it with saline before we peel."

He took a moment to step out, intending to fetch a couple bags, but, when he saw one of the nurses coming, asked in his most persuasive tones instead, then went back to wait with his still-sterile gloves.

"Listen," she said when he sat, looking down at him with what he could only dub chagrin, "I'm sorry that I was so cranky with you earlier in the cafeteria. You didn't want to participate—that's not a sin. I just—there was a thing in the ER today and I sorta let it color my mood. I don't want to be the kind of person who judges someone by the actions of another, and that's what I did. So, I'm sorry."

He didn't need to ask who she'd judged him by. His brother had been at Sutcliffe a shorter time than she had—since he'd recovered from the shooting and the charming brother he'd known had become this grating, ever-irritated guy no one wanted to be around. Fortunately for him, Lyons was still a great doctor, even if his bedside manner was arsey.

"What did Lyons do?"

She went a little bug-eyed and then shook her head. "It's… I don't want to gossip or talk about anyone. There was a thing, and I got upset, and then I sorta took it out on you and you didn't deserve that. Even if you did earn a little of my ire by not caring whether the kids were disappointed. Nothing that meant rudeness and I know I was rude."

"You weren't that rude," he said, then stopped when the RN he'd begged supplies from came back with the saline, a basin for him to wash her knee over and a gown to cover his clothes. He stood, she helped him carefully into it and then helped Angel shift back on the bed so she could lie with her knee over the basin.

The stuff about the kids he'd leave alone. He

cared whether the kids were disappointed, but he had placed it lower in the priorities than his desire to not continue this *thing*. It wasn't a black-or-white issue, it just became a gray he could live with. At least before. Maybe not now. There would already be children to reassure that Dr. Angel was all right. Especially Jenna. And he'd have to do that because he was going to write her off work tomorrow, make her rest the knee for the weekend, whether she wanted to or not. Call it his good deed, even if she was unhappy about it.

When they were alone again, before he unwrapped her leg or doused it with saline, he leaned over to make sure and look her in the eye. "Are you off this weekend?"

"Yes. I work tomorrow, then I'm off Saturday and Sunday."

"You're off tomorrow," he corrected, and before she could protest said, "You'll thank me in the morning when it's burning like a knife wound and you don't want to do anything but sit and read that paperback in your lumpy satchel."

Her mouth screwed to the side and he nodded when she didn't argue. "You don't have to tell me what happened with Lyons, and what I'm going to say isn't an excuse for any bad behavior, but do you know what happened at his last hospital?"

He could see her working through any gossip she might have heard.

"I know there was something bad at his last hospital, but I don't really have the kind of relationships that make me someone people want to tell stuff to."

That was something else he wanted to ask about but knew better for the moment. It wasn't his business, and it was probably *personal.* People were probably paying extra close attention to her now, to both of them, because she didn't hang out with anyone and he was known to... enjoy hanging out with a lot of different women. Just not any from work. Ever. Which was why he still struggled to keep reminding himself that she was not someone he should become used to hanging out with or indulge the fond feelings that had wormed into his chest tonight at the rink.

But Lyons? He could at least give her some insight into his brother's unfortunate situation, even if it wouldn't inspire her to tell him what had happened.

"Last Christmas, he worked at a hospital north of the city, and one of his coworkers, someone who was having domestic problems, took up his offer to help her get away from her husband. She came to the hospital on Christmas Eve, and when they were speaking, her husband came and shot them both. She didn't survive. Lyons barely did. When he recovered enough to return to work, I talked him into coming here instead. He's a great medical mind, always has been, but his people skills have deteriorated."

She leaned up on her elbows, her brows pinched so hard the line that formed between them could've passed for the Grand Canyon on a topographical map. "That's awful. No one told me that. Does he speak with someone?"

Therapy. Something Wolfe had tried a few times to get going but failed. "He went to the few sessions the hospital required to clear him, but no."

"Does he talk about it with you?" she asked, and that was when Wolfe knew he needed to stop this conversation.

He reached for the saline and opened it up. "No. We're not a close family."

It was the only answer he had to give. They'd never been close, but still, they were brothers. Wolfe had come to New York at Lyons's request and as a way to get out from under their parents. It sounded like a small thing, but Wolfe had known it for what it was: a protective, brotherly instinct. One Lyons barely let him return even when he'd been critically wounded and needed protecting.

"Oh." The small sound made him look at her face again, needing for some reason to see if that was a sound that meant judgment or something else.

Regret. That was what he saw in her deep, understanding eyes. She knew what it was like to not have that family closeness. Which explained why she wasn't moving to Atlanta to be close to family. Didn't explain why she didn't have any friends here, but he really couldn't ask that—he already had a literal wound to deal with, and no clue on emotional wound treatment.

"Ready?" he asked instead.

She nodded, and then sat up better so she could watch him. She had to watch, she'd said. Whatever else she'd claimed about knowing he was a good doctor, she didn't trust easily.

Watching was her only defense.

And distance was his. Three days without seeing her should help him too.

* * *

The next morning came and went, Wolfe's morning surgeries were blessedly without complications. Now to change, make rounds, visit with Jenna and family to reassure them about Angel's knee, and go home.

Today was supposed to be distancing and mellowing to this struggle of attraction Angel had triggered in him, but the way his thoughts kept returning to her revealed the flaw in his plan.

Because of her knee, they were in the clear through the weekend for anything new to broadcast, but the relief he'd expected failed to materialize.

He'd just shed his scrub top when he heard the door open and tilted his head to see who'd come in.

A petite blonde with a sleek ponytail met his gaze and he saw the usual spark of interest there that he always saw.

Reynolds.

God, not today.

The easy mood he liked to ride at work had already been corrupted by his own inability to control his thoughts. He shouldn't be concerned how Angel was doing. He shouldn't keep wondering if she had someone there at her apartment helping her out, or if she had to hobble through alone. They needed this time apart for him to cool down.

He had no patience left for Reynolds today.

Angel returned to work after three days restlessly resting her knee in her quiet apartment.

It was a nice apartment, she supposed. But small. A party of one didn't need that much room, but when her playground had been mountains, the progressively smaller living spaces that led to New York real estate made being inside feel claustrophobic if she was forced to spend too much time indoors.

The biggest feature of her decor was her bookshelves. She liked to read, but the truth was she felt that loneliness that had been the main catalyst for her decision to leave New York even more acutely.

The two evenings she'd spent out with Wolfe, even begrudgingly, even though the second had ended with stitches, had been the best times she'd had since arriving in New York. Since longer, if she was being honest. It tempted her. He'd been so kind; would he believe her if she told him the unlikely truth? If she had someone to stand by her, a friend to back her up if it all caught up with her and the hospital decided she wasn't worth the hassle, that would be enough to take the risk.

No sooner had the thought occurred than the sinking feeling came in her middle. Would she ever truly learn that lesson? So stupid.

Probably a side-effect of all this alone time her knee forced on her. Extra-long weekends? Not good for her. Despite her knee alternating between aching and burning, she'd rather be at the hospital. Which was how she wound up rising extra early to visit Jenna on Monday before her own day began.

When she arrived, the first thing she saw was a sign on Jenna's door denoting infection, along with boxes of paper gowns and gloves, and a posting about the isolation protocol.

Dread sinking in her middle, she shook out a gown, donned it and the gloves, then slipped into the quiet room.

She knew by the protocol what it was: a hospital-acquired infection. Not something to do with the surgery, just another thing for Jenna's already beleaguered little body to fight off.

The one bright spot was the lack of masks in the supplies, which told her it wasn't airborne. It was spread by touch.

The lights were mostly off, but the one above Jenna's bed lit the ceiling well enough for her to see Mrs. Lindsey in the chair beside Jenna's bed, and when she focused on Jenna, even in the low light she could see her pallor rivaled the bedsheets.

"Dr. Angel," she greeted, voice small, but smile still there. Unlike the day Angel had found her sulking and refusing to eat, today she could tell Jenna wanted to show her usual cheer, but she just couldn't quite get there. "How's your knee?"

"Healing very well. Dr. Wolfe took good care of me," Angel said, letting her eyes take in the rest of the room, which only increased the heaviness in her chest. The decorations that had been put up days before were gone. No tree. No stuffed bears in Christmas sweaters. All that remained were the twinkle lights around the television, currently not twinkling.

One questioning look at Mrs. Lindsey got the diagnosis. *"C. Dif."*

Damn.

"Did they start her on IV antibiotics?" Angel asked as she headed to see what was currently hanging on Jenna's IV pole. Just saline.

"They bring it twice a day. Started yesterday morning," Mrs. Lindsey informed her, and Angel had to work to keep the sigh welling inside her from bursting forth.

"What am I gonna do with you, kid?" she asked Jenna, taking the risk and pulling one of her gloves off so she could take Jenna's hand without a vinyl barrier.

"Wheelchair race," Jenna suggested, "with Dr. Wolfe. For the next video stream."

Not about her, not exactly. She squeezed the little hand and went along with the subject. "How is that related to Christmas?"

"I don't know, you could sing 'Jingle Bells' or something."

She couldn't help but grin. Even weak and exhausted, Jenna was still all-in on the Christmas streams. "I think wheelchair races might be a little insensitive to our patients who have to get around in a wheelchair, honey. I wouldn't want to make them feel bad."

"But you can't run around now. Dr. Wolfe said you have to let your knee heal without strain and activity."

Apparently, Wolfe had come to give them the same speech he'd given her. And in Jenna's mind, Angel could have a wheelchair race if she needed a wheelchair to help her. Made sense.

Sort of. But it still wasn't going to happen. "I'll keep that in mind."

"When's the next one?"

"I don't know yet. I just got back from my forced rest, and I came to see you before anyone else."

"But you're going to do another one, right?" Jenna asked, apparently needing to hear it.

Angel hadn't spoken to Wolfe about that either. Hadn't spoken to him at all since he'd so dutifully and gallantly tended her after the fall and driven her home afterward. She'd refused to let him inside her tiny, book-crammed apartment, but he'd got her there in one piece.

As if summoned by her thinking of him, a knock came at the door and Wolfe breezed in. "Morning, ladies."

He made eye contact with Angel a moment too long, and then looked pointedly at her bare hand.

Yes, she was breaking protocol.

"I'm getting the stink-eye from Dr. Wolfe for breaking protocol, honey. You tell him what you want to do next. No wheelchairs."

With a final squeeze, she went over to the sink, peeled off the other glove and chucked both before giving her hands a vigorous wash and donning a new pair of gloves. As isolation required. Funny that soap and water was better at containing such an infection than alcohol.

When she returned to the bed, Wolfe was holding the hand she'd abandoned, his own hand out of the glove now. Angel moved to the side and hung out, listening shamelessly to Wolfe's talk about the virus.

"I know you don't want to eat," he was saying, "and even though you have a very valid reason for that, you still need to get nutrients into you. Your body needs fuel to heal."

"Even water makes me have to go potty. It's awful."

Poor kid. It was a virulent, terrible infection.

"He's right, honey." They went through a long discussion about what to do to help get through, and just when Angel thought they were managing, Jenna changed the subject.

"Dr. Angel is under the mistletoe."

One simple statement, and both their heads jerked back to spy the little sliding hook upon which the mistletoe had been hung. The mistletoe Angel had forgotten about and which also hadn't been removed during the sterilization.

Wolfe looked at Angel, and then back at Jenna. "Tell me this isn't another barter, darlin'."

Her heart stopped. Just stopped. When she

opened her mouth to casually mention her sudden heart failure, it slammed back into full throttle and the sound that escaped her open mouth more closely resembled a gasp than a word.

An unfortunately timed gasp.

All eyes swiveled to her, heat flashing on her cheeks as she forced her mouth closed.

"No. I don't want to eat." Jenna saved her by speaking. She shook her head with as much energy as Angel had seen from her. "But the mistletoe rule says you kiss the girl under the mistletoe. They took out the rest of my decorations because they might be infected and couldn't be cleaned good enough. Mom had to throw the tree and things away because they said the only way to kill it is bleach, and if you bleach a Christmas tree, it'll be ruined."

It went on. Jenna was upset about her initial illness, as anyone would be, and it just kept compounding. First, she couldn't go to their traditional family outing, then all her Christmas decorations—her white Christmas tree with pink and rose gold ornaments—were taken away. She wanted her way about something, and Wolfe was arguing because…she was so objectionable to kiss? Or maybe because she'd gasped, and he'd mistaken her reaction for horror?

By the time they got to another round of him saying no, Angel had had enough. She tapped his shoulder twice, and, when he looked at her, grabbed his cheeks and popped a quick, chaste kiss on his lips.

That was what she'd intended, at least.

Kiss. Back off. Give the kid something she wanted for once. Prove she wasn't an unkissable leper. And then be done with it. Nothing to see, move along.

Instead, the instant her lips touched his, what she could only call a jolt speared her lips and began spreading out over her face, down her neck, over her chest with her second possible cardiac arrest of the morning.

Jenna laughed. "You're supposed to kiss his cheek!"

His cheek? There went her third heart attack in the past minute.

"Oh." God, she was a mess. And she needed to get the heck out of there. "Uh, I'll remember for next time. But my shift'll be startin'."

In a while, hopefully long enough for the red-hot nature of her cheeks to diminish to where it was only powerful enough to heat a city block, not the whole danged city.

She washed up and made it to the hallway in

record time, her mouth still buzzing from the kiss. It wasn't static. Not actually a shock. It wasn't as if she'd dragged her feet all through the hospital and built a charge that only found a ground when her lips touched his, but whatever it was left her sparking all over, and overly aware of her own mouth as she'd never been aware of her mouth.

She'd gotten about ten heart-racing paces down the hallway into another dimension when Wolfe caught up with her.

With a steel grip, he captured her elbow and dragged her into the sunken alcove that housed a phone held over from the old paging system, turning her as she moved until she was sandwiched between him and the wall.

Should she say something? But how could she say anything when she'd just forgotten how to think thoughts?

He stood so close, the heat from him canceled out the cold wall at her back, leaving her with nothing but visceral reactions. The effect of prolonged loneliness, and overly familiar contact with the object of her secret crush. It was a mess, and she was a mess to have taken it to that level.

But he wasn't speaking either. She lifted her

gaze from the rapid pulse throbbing at the hollow of his throat to those gorgeous blue eyes.

She opened her mouth to apologize, but what she saw in his eyes stopped her cold.

He wasn't angry. He was...interested? He'd felt something, maybe not that obsessive, will-sapping full-body sparkles, but *something*.

As he leaned in the strong grip on her arm softened, released and slipped to her waist to grip in a kind of rolling caress.

His breath feathered her cheeks, and her own came faster in response. The last remnants of her spontaneous kiss roared back to a buzz that drowned out everything else.

He was going to kiss her. Not a quick kiss to placate a patient. A real kiss. The kind of kiss that she'd been imagining from him for the past eleven months.

He licked his lips. She licked hers. And his gaze held, pupils so dilated the icy blue was almost gone. It was down to that nearly indigo band around the outside, and the black pupils that held promises she couldn't even begin to name.

The tip of his nose brushed her cheek and her eyes drifted shut as her body instinctively strained forward and up, closer, closer...

"You two, wait until you're after hours." A woman's voice broke through the haze, snapping her away from him.

Wolfe jerked back and let go of her, and she realized then that her legs had gone stupid. She had to grab the phone shelf to keep from sagging to the floor like some boneless bag of clichéd idiocy.

He caught up with who was speaking before she did. "Margot. We're not dating."

She snorted, making her doubts clear, then moved on.

It was a children's ward, but Angel took one comfort in the fact that there wasn't a single child in sight. Just the hallway. Just Margot and Wolfe and her, the confused mute who couldn't think of anything to say and who held her eyes especially wide open now to keep from doing that blinking thing again.

He looked at her, the anticipation she'd seen there gone, replaced by a new look of irritation. Was he upset that he'd almost kissed her or that they'd gotten caught?

She didn't know because he didn't say anything, just stepped out of the alcove and began down the hallway.

Which was when she remembered that she'd

wanted to speak with him earlier. As fast as her leg would allow, she scooted from the alcove and called, "Wolfe? Dr. McKeag?"

That stopped him. He half turned to look at her, his jaw clenched repeatedly, and in profile she could see how rapid the rise and fall of his chest was—breathing fast—but he said nothing.

"Will you come speak with me later? About another outing?"

"Lunch." Single-word answer, then he kept going the direction he had been, stiff as she'd never seen him.

Lunch. She'd better eat before he got there. If her automatic body processes kept trying to fail around him, she'd choke to death if she tried to eat. The Heimlich Maneuver was not the way she wanted to get his arms around her. Because she did want that, she had to admit. Even if she wasn't able to share anything else, she wanted him.

And he wanted her too, heaven help her.

CHAPTER SEVEN

"I BOUGHT US ugly Christmas sweaters," were the first words out of Angel's mouth when Wolfe approached her table in the cafeteria.

No greeting. No variation in the table she preferred even. It was the same empty table he'd found her at earlier in the week.

As awkward as he'd expected this meeting to be, his wandering mind had it revolving around resisting attraction, and the pull of intense, longing looks. Uncomfortable meaningful pauses.

But she'd flipped it before he'd even sat down by using the wrong word. The exactly most wrong word. The word that had been ringing around in his head since he'd almost kissed her in the hallway earlier. *Us.*

It helped dissipate that desire to kiss her.

Grabbing the closest chair, he sat and held up one finger, not sure what prompted this bizarre, instant confession, but addressing it before he went forward seemed the safest thing. "Angel, you're saying 'us' a little too easily. We're not an *us*."

She'd looked nervous before, but now her cheeks started to turn red, and she did the worst thing he could think of, just nodding at his words, without saying anything else.

The sweater talk had been her wall to hide behind to avoid the subject of her earlier embarrassment, and he'd shorted her out by taking it head-on.

This turning down of colleagues was becoming a weekly thing. The difference this time was he felt guilty about it; he'd never had guilt over Reynolds.

Her gaze drifted back to the table, but her eyes stretched wider, alert, as if she expected an attack. What the hell had Lyons said to her?

"I assume you want to wear the jumpers to something?" he asked, gentling his voice and trying to get back to the reason she'd wanted to talk to begin with.

It wasn't a nod, and it wasn't a shake for the negative—her head just sort of bobbled around in a way that didn't commit to anything. "Or work. Or not. It's fine if you don't want to."

Too forceful. He had to be forceful with Reynolds, who was always grabbing, but Angel needed a lighter touch. She wasn't exactly grabbing. Her actions seemed more hapless and mostly accidental seduction than the whole… breast-baring thing.

"I'll wear it. It's fine." He leaned back in his chair and tried to start whatever conversation she'd wanted to have, let her speak before he said his piece. "Were the jumpers what you wanted to talk about?"

She picked up her fork and pushed a lingering bit of lettuce around her empty bowl, distracting herself. Fidgeting, but with a fork.

"I wanted to tell you that you don't have to keep doing this with me. I know you don't want to, and I'll tell Alberts that what I did, that it crossed a line and you don't want to and shouldn't have to…you know, spend all this time with me now."

Definitely too forceful. He tilted his head to try and catch her gaze, but she looked so intently in the empty bowl that he had to touch her arm to get her to look at him, and even then it was more of a quick, furtive glance that lasted a bare second than connecting eye contact.

"You don't have to do that. You don't have to apologize and get yourself into trouble. I almost kissed you in the hall, and I guarantee it wasn't going to be so chaste as yours."

"But you're upset," she whispered, and turned her gaze back to the bowl as if it was helping her, because that wobble in her voice said she was more upset than she was trying to pretend.

"I'm not upset like that. I don't know what the word is for what I am. Frustrated?" Telling her the truth would be easier. On him, at least. Maybe her. "I have a code. About work. About dating at work. About bringing drama to work."

"Which is what this is, right? I mean, I made it awkward."

"No." Touching her hadn't helped, but he wanted her to look at him. It was hard enough to read her expression when she looked at him dead-on, but in profile? Nothing. He nudged her foot with his. "You just shined a spotlight on the fact that I already was fighting the urge to break my own code with you."

"I try to be so careful and deliberate about what I say and do, but then I get…" Her words trailed off and she shook her head. "I don't know. My mouth gets ahead of my mind, I guess other parts of me too. Just doesn't happen very often, and has been happening a lot the past week, mostly with Jenna but also with you. Maybe I'm burned out."

"How old are you?"

"Thirty-two."

"You're not burned out," he said, then asked, "Is this your first full-time position?"

She nodded, then winced and shook her head. "I had another job when I first got to New York, but it didn't last."

"Why not?"

"Interfering ex," she mumbled, studiously staring at a flaw on the tabletop.

"You had to quit to get away from him?"

She shook her head, and the look of embarrassment that passed over her face made the earlier incident look like nothing.

"He got you fired?"

"Before I even got through the first week of in-service they required for all Emergency personnel," she muttered, lifting one shoulder as if it didn't matter even while her face broadcast an entirely different story. "Let's talk about the next...what did you call it? Shenanigan?"

Fired before she'd even hit the floor? Which meant Jenna was her first patient in her first real, full-time job. And she was far from home, and struggling to fit in, and recently betrayed by someone she trusted—at least that was the only situation he could imagine, knowing even a little bit about her. There was more to the story, a shadow he didn't want to ask about, but this was enough to draw some conclusions. And he didn't know how to ask her about that any more than he knew how to ask Lyons the things *someone* needed to ask him. Not without pushing him further away.

One thing he knew without asking: this was what kept her so quiet and reserved, protecting herself or beating herself up over it somehow. All he could do was ignore it.

"Christmas shenanigans. Right. Tell me what you want to do next. Alberts wants us to keep it up, do things he can use for a PR campaign, but I'm not doing this for him. I'm doing it for the kids, and you are too. We need to do stuff the kids will enjoy. So, what's your idea? Does it fit that?"

Refocusing the conversation seemed to help, the shenanigans had united them, after all, but, damn, he wanted to ask about the ex. He'd had some spectacular break-ups, but none that ended with quite that much drama. It was almost Mc-Keag-worthy.

"I was thinking of a couple things. Decorating gingerbread houses could be fun. Funny too, because I'm a terrible cook, and, unless you've been to pastry school, you probably are too. The next day, we could bring in gingerbread men purchased from a bakery, so as to be edible. If we can get it cleared by Dietary."

Gingerbread? Frosting?

"That works." He had no business in a kitchen. "But we're agreed the rest need to be something amusing to the kids, something they'll enjoy. Not whatever Alberts has hashed up. That's the only way I'm continuing."

She nodded again, but still looked...offended? No. That wasn't it. Upset. Hurt. She looked hurt, and it wasn't only the talk of the ex from hell. It was still him, and the wrong foot he'd started this out on.

Even Lyons had only made her angry. Wolfe had never in his life had a successful relationship, and he was sure he couldn't. It wasn't that he hadn't tried, he'd just never succeeded— whether because he was inherently selfish or what, he couldn't say. What he knew was that look in her eyes, and the way her soft lips turned down ever so slightly at the corners, made him want to kiss her just so she wouldn't look like that anymore.

Given what he knew, maybe a friendship could be possible. She certainly seemed in no hurry to get involved with a *relationship* after whatever happened.

And she was leaving soon...

She took long enough to answer that he touched her arm again, just to get her going. "Angel? Is that short for Angela?"

"Angelica." She answered that at least. "My other idea was decorating a tree, or a Santa visit. Something like that. We could hire a Santa to come to the floor, but he'd need to be instructed on all the protocols. Doubt a typical mall Santa would be up for handling the children with special requirements. Would you want to dress as Santa?"

It was an opening he couldn't pass up.

"Would you dress as an elf or Mrs. Santa?"

"I don't know—either?"

"Elf," he said, and then grinned. "With pointy ears or the deal is off."

She almost smiled then; the corners of her mouth were at least flat, or maybe had a slight upward tilt. "If I can find them. Or Mr. Spock ears if nothing else."

"Vulcan elf, even better." Even hotter, his mind argued. "And a Christmas tree? Here?"

"No, I was thinking your place. It'd probably make them happy to see where you live."

Having her in his house would only ratchet up the temptation. "Why not your place?"

"My place is very spartan. And small. I mostly have bedroom furniture, a couch and bookshelves everywhere. I don't even have a dining table, just a desk where I often eat."

"Already packed up for your move?"

She paused, back to weighing her words before speaking. He'd been demoted.

"Never really settled, I guess. Maybe I'm just stuck in the resident mindset where everything is temporary. Or maybe it just felt temporary here because I don't fit."

Dammit, he was going to have to ask. It was inevitable, because as much as he wanted to get some distance, he didn't. It pulled at him in equal measures. Was this idea about the jerk she'd dated? Could he get the guy's name to go smash him in the face?

"Why is it you don't think you fit in?"

"I don't know. Almost a year and I'm still practically brand new. Tomorrow could be my first day, every day could be my first day except I know where everything is and who I'm supposed to report to or contact for information

for this or that. I'm just not suited to New York,
I guess. Which is too bad."

"That's a non-answer."

"There are things about me that…people
wouldn't approve of."

"Another non-answer."

"It's not."

"Whatever it is can't be that bad."

She sighed hard, then waved a hand. "Fine, but
I still don't want to tell you. I barely know you."

"Fair enough," he conceded, but said directly,
so there could be no mistake, "But you're suited
to the job, Angelica."

When he used her full name, her head snapped
up and she looked at him; none of the sadness
or wariness that had been lingering in her eyes
was there when he said her name. "I don't know
the last time someone called me Angelica."

"Family?"

Shut up, idiot. No more prying.

"I don't think so." Her gaze drifted to the side
and he could see she was searching her memory. And when she found it, he knew then too,
that line that had appeared between her brows
softened and faded.

Let it go. Stop digging. He'd be angry if she

dug into his problems. But he asked anyway. "Who was it?"

"Ah…" It was a verbal tic, she didn't really want to tell him who, but, after a moment, seemed to wrestle with something and finally said, "A social worker."

Social worker. An ex who got her fired for something. Gods.

He *knew* he shouldn't have asked. Now what did he do with that? Leave it lying there? Act as if it never happened and move on? Would she even tell him if he asked?

Unlikely.

After several long seconds, he made a noise that brought her gaze back to his. "I like you, so I'm going to be blunt. I don't know what I'm supposed to do when you reluctantly mention a social worker from a long time ago, but you basically already said you don't trust me."

"I said I don't know you."

"Do I pretend it never happened, so you don't feel awkward?"

"I'm sorry," she said immediately. "This is getting messed up."

"Agreed. But now I have to ask, why were you speaking to a social worker who called you by your first name?"

She winced. "There were some things. No one's childhood is perfect, right?"

Another dodge. No one's childhood was perfect, but there was a certain level of imperfect that required *social workers*.

Stop now.

He jerked his hand through the air, cutting himself off more than her, and returned to the subject he understood. "My place is fine for stuff. I guess. I wouldn't want people thinking it's too ostentatious or something."

"Where do you live?"

He gave a short laugh. "I live above my pay grade, Angel."

And avoided her full name.

"Where?"

"Tribeca, in an old converted church with a small parsonage on the side," he said, and then tilted his head in a half-shrug. "Which I suppose would be a good place for Christmas stuff. Let's just do it all at my place, the gingerbread and the tree. I've got a big, never-used kitchen. All bright and modern, lots of counterspace, and two ovens, I think? The sanctuary was split into two floors, and the upstairs loft has space in front of the big rose window. It's not one of those windows with a story in the glass, but old stained glass, so it's churchy. Could put the tree there to frame in the window. People would probably think that was pretty."

"Where were you going to put your tree? There?"

He shook his head. "I don't do trees. I'll have to get one and the stuff for it. But if we do the gingerbread stuff first, that gives time for the tree stuff to be delivered."

"Why don't you do a tree when you have all that room?"

"I told you, I don't like Christmas."

"Because of Lyons's shooting?"

"No. I never liked it. We didn't do Christmas when I was growing up. Just never was a thing for me. Or just something that failed to live up to expectations." He also didn't talk about his family, a survival tactic from his childhood that had carried over, long past the time when people asked pointed, not innocent questions.

She digested this for a couple of seconds, confusion growing on her face. "But I thought your family was moneyed?"

The question implied not having money was the only reason she could think of that people wouldn't do Christmas. Maybe that was the cause of her need for a social worker. And a reason for her to not like Christmas. And perhaps why she didn't speak of her family. Was she one of those unfortunate little children who shuffled around foster care or group homes where money was always tight?

Did he even want to answer her about his own Christmas-shaped issues?

No, this was already a lot of prying into personal business, but it felt as if he had to give her something in return. Even the score, or at least let her feel on more equal footing, because it was clear neither one of them knew how to work and play all that well with others.

"My family comes from a long line of wealth, true. But money never made anyone a good person, lass. My parents are both a complete mess, and our family has been immersed in one salacious scandal after another. Neither Lyons nor I associate with them beyond the odd call every few years."

"Salacious?" she repeated, prompting more information. Information he'd really rather not give.

"Public affairs, extremely indecent behavior, instigated but never completed divorces with as much drama and child-shaped weaponry as you can pack into it." He shrugged. "It was a lot to deal with. Still is, as I understand it. You want to know more? Do an internet search for them. You'll find lots of gritty details about my mum and dad, Tavia and Ewan McKeag."

Let her learn more about them without him having to go over it. Maybe she'd understand his hesitance to get anywhere near drama after having a good read, even if he already regretted telling her. And maybe she'd feel him more trustworthy if she knew something about his own closet skeletons. In Scotland, it was difficult to get away from talk about them, and the distance, both geographical and emotional, prompted his escape, but this once he could revisit it.

Her frown didn't convince him she believed him, or said she had trouble picturing it.

"When do you want to make them? Do we need special supplies?" he asked, to get back on the subject before lunch ended.

"I'll take care of that. And speak with Dietary about whether it's okay to bring in gingerbread men for the whole ward." She went with it.

Get the information, get it all sorted out, get her to stop looking quite so lost. "Will it take long?"

Really, he was off his game with her. He could

always make people smile. Finding the unserious in the serious? He could always do that. But
today he'd had to rely on a confessional about
his parents' depraved natures being broadcast to
half of Europe on the regular, and this morning
he'd almost kissed her—would have if they'd
not been interrupted.

Clearly, he was out of his depth with her.

"No. I already did the legwork—a bakery to
bake the house parts, make the frosting, and edible gingerbread men to bring in."

She spoke at length about the plans, and all
he had to do was supply the location and show
up. Tomorrow evening.

"We'll wear the ugly jumpers for that. Or
maybe the tree. You decide." He stood up, ready
to put some space between them, and maybe
grab a sandwich before he got back to work.
But before he could make himself go, he looked
down at her again and asked, "Are you all right?"

Her smile was a little tight, but much better
than that little sad bird mouth she'd had for the
first half of their conversation, and she nodded.

It would have to be enough. He didn't know
how to do more. Never had.

CHAPTER EIGHT

ANGEL GAWKED FROM the back seat of the cab as it stopped in front of a church in Tribeca.

This couldn't be it. Wolfe had said it was a small church converted to a house, but the building the cabbie stopped in front of would've been a regular, or big, church back home. The kind about two hundred people would attend Sunday worship. Somewhere she would've gone to pray that the mistletoe fiasco never be spoken of. Only fancier.

"Are you sure this is the place?" she asked, fumbling for her phone to double-check.

The cabbie gestured out of the window. "Do you know him?"

There was Wolfe, striding down the walk to meet her. Her stomach bottomed out.

She'd been half hoping this would all end in some funny mix-up where she couldn't find his place and had to take all her cookie paraphernalia home to eat the equivalent of three gingerbread houses alone, because sometimes a girl needed to eat her feelings. Especially when her feelings were stupid.

"Yeah, I know him." She sighed, unable to help herself, and paid just as the door opened.

Wolfe leaned through to look over what she'd brought and eyed the stack of boxes on the other side of her, reminding her of the tree-lighting, when he'd flirted without reservation, and ducked into her cab to kiss her cheek.

Now he looked all business. "Need a hand?"

There was no getting out of this now. The only things she could afford to destroy were the things she'd brought with her, and whatever remained of her self-esteem.

"Need two." She carefully shuffled half the boxes to his hands, then took the remaining half for herself, and climbed out. "Be careful, they're carefully wrapped, but they're still cookies. I got enough for three houses, one for you, one for me and one for spare parts when we break everything."

"Good thinking." He nudged the door closed with one leg and then nodded sideways toward the door to his churchy house. "Let's go put these in the kitchen and I'll give you a tour. See if you like the place I picked to put the tree."

She felt herself already bristling—what did she know about that kind of thing? "It's your house, we'll put it where you want to put it."

"I told you, I don't do Christmas. I don't really care where it goes." He carefully opened the door, and she was at least momentarily mollified to see that he didn't have a butler, or a private doorman to handle the lowly tasks, like turning doorknobs, for him. If he hadn't said his kitchen had never been used, on seeing the house she'd have expected him to have a live-in private chef.

Even having steadied herself to expect opulence and given herself a stern lecture about not touching anything, the instant she stepped through the heavily carved, solid wooden door, she froze.

It wasn't garish—despite having been a church, there was no trace of gilding, and it didn't need it. There were white walls and gorgeous, dark walnut beams and woodwork. Just from where she stood, to the left she could see into what was probably once the sanctuary, and there were marble columns. An archway the other direction was one of those pointed-top curvy ones that she couldn't picture gothic cathedrals without, and which probably had a name. A name that *he* knew. A name she would've probably learned had she not been intimidated by art history classes after the first and only mandatory one she'd been required to take as an undergraduate.

"Angel?" His voice was gentle, but full of questions. Then he actually asked a question. "What's wrong?"

And directly ahead, there was an elevator. Good God Almighty, the man had an elevator. He was not a normal person, and neither was she. They represented such drastically opposite ends of the spectrum that it made this all worse somehow. As if she should just be there to clean the chimney, otherwise she didn't belong.

"Is this the house?" The plush furniture she spied where there should be pews said house, but her feet stayed stuck by the door, her fingers curled into the boxes so hard they dented.

He put his boxes down on a table near the door and came to take hers away. "This is it. Let's get these into the kitchen."

"No! Let's go to the other house. You said there was a parsonage? Let's use that house. This is...this is..."

"Angel?" He repeated her name after she repeated herself at least seven hundred times, breaking the cycle and pulling her big eyes to him.

She knew they were big, because they were opened too wide and starting to feel dry and hard to focus. Then there was the clammy feeling blooming over her whole body that probably meant sweating for no reason.

"There is a parsonage. It's a guest house. Lyons stayed there when he was recovering, and a few friends have visited and stayed there."

"So, it's furnished. Good! Good... Let's go there. Let's film there instead."

"The parsonage has a really small kitchen." Wolfe shook his head, and he didn't even seem to be trying to get rid of the concern she saw there.

Unlike her. She was doing everything short of using her fingers to squish her features to remove the freakish bent she knew they'd taken, return to something more normal or at least less cartoonishly horrified.

"We're going to need a lot of room to put these together. And there's better lighting here to film by."

Film. Right. Right. They were going to live stream. For the kids. For Jenna, the twelve-year-old with stars in her eyes, who would love to see Wolfe's big, fancy house.

"What's freaking you out? Is it because it's a church? Did you have a bad experience in a church?"

There! He'd given her an out. She could con her way out of this, and that was a lesson from her early, family-led education: when you were drowning or about to be caught, use whatever lifeline was available.

She could just *lie*.

Lots of people had bad experiences in churches, probably. But she couldn't explain this reaction outside something really traumatic, which was a Big Lie. She didn't like Big Lies. Little ones were bad enough.

"No." She forced her suddenly stiff hands to the buttons on her coat and started working them open. Normal actions. Civilized people took off their coats when entering someone's home. This was Wolfe's home. And if the universe wanted to draw a line around exactly why her crush on him was especially dumb, this was it. The man was so far out of her league he shouldn't even know her name. He shouldn't have to mix with someone like her.

"What is it?"

"Why do you think I should be so much better at deciding where to put your Christmas tree when this is where you live?" Was her voice high? It sounded high. "I mean, I've never had a Christmas tree that wasn't cut down in the middle of the night from someone else's private property and which we had to move furniture out of the house to even make a space to set up. So, you know…just…you pick where the tree goes."

And she'd never wanted one since. That wasn't what she'd meant to say, but that was what came out. She got the coat off, then looked around for a place to put it, the panic still there but starting to sting more because of embarrassment. If she'd built up any good karma with her work and trying to lead a good life, then how fast she'd babbled all that out would make it hard for him to understand. His brother had implied that she and her Tennessee mountaintop people were practically incomprehensible anyway.

He took her words without comment but stepped to her and disengaged her hands from the wool collar she was wrenching into a misshapen mess and took the three steps needed to carry him to what was apparently a coat closet. A coat closet with a fancy pointed arch on the top of the door and wrought-iron hinges like a medieval castle.

"Here." He left the boxes of cookies on the table, took her hand and led her stiff-legged through the fancy archway to some stairs. The stairs were closed in and carpeted, they looked like normal stairs. Just up. A bend in the middle past which she couldn't see. White walls. Very nice wood railing. And, most importantly, nothing to break.

Halfway up, closed in the small space, the panic started to fade back into a weird buzzing at the base of her skull. And warmth in her hand. His hand, big and warm, squeezing and relaxing, squeezing and relaxing in the way she did when trying to soothe a patient or worried parent. It worked. Provided enough distraction to get her out of her own head.

"Wolfe?" she said when they reached the landing, before making the turn to continue up. The man had seen enough, she could either let him jump to conclusions that could be worse than the truth or tell him something now that her brain had resumed function.

"I'm a little intimidated by fancy things. All day I've been telling myself *just don't break anything*. Just don't break anything. Like parents everywhere say when they take their children into shops with glassware around. Don't break *nothing* at Wolfe's fancy house."

He kept squeezing her hand but nodded and gave a little tug so she stood closer, not commenting on another grammar slip; they were emotional tells he was growing grateful for. "I don't have a lot of breakables lying around, but if you break something, what do you think I'm going to do?"

"I don't know. Sue me for breaking a Ming Dynasty vase. Vaze? Vace? However you say it."

"Do I look like a Ming Dynasty vase sort of bloke?"

She gestured helplessly around, then ended up pointing an accusing finger at him. "You live in a church mansion. What if I fell through the stained-glass window? You have a stained-glass window in your house, and it's probably bigger than my whole apartment."

"We'll skip the tour, then. Go back downstairs. I'll blindfold you and lead you to the kitchen so if you break anything in transit, it's my fault."

"Ha ha."

"Or I can carry you. Toss you over my shoulder, then you can look at my bum the whole way, and I know you wouldn't hate that."

"Wolfe!" She squawked his name and, although she left her hand still tucked into his, shoved at his chest with her poking hand. Fat lot of good it did—he didn't even wobble. "I don't need a close-up view of your butt. This has nothing to do with you. It's the same feeling that comes every time I think about that danged ball we're supposed to go to. I don't know how to explain it better than that."

"I get it," he said, the teasing light in his eyes dimming. "You didn't have much growing up, right?"

She nodded.

"If you don't have money to pay for accidents, the idea of breaking anything is scary." He filled in her silence, adding, "There's nothing at the ball valuable enough to worry over. They have insurance against roving bands of unruly southern belles."

"I'm not a southern belle," she said softly, letting go of his hand in favor of the railing to go back downstairs. Then under her breath, "I'm one of *those* Conleys from Tarpin Holler."

"What was that?" He was just behind her on the stairs.

She stopped at the foot of the stairs, gestured

for him to move ahead of her and lied. "I said I want to follow."

"You said *foller*," he corrected, but, when he moved past, took her hand again. "You know, things that happen make us the balls of neuroses we always end up. But they aren't stone. You can get over this by spending time in my fancy house."

He couldn't understand, and she didn't have the heart to explain it to him. Instead, she just walked where he led. At least he hadn't been put off by *"foller."*

There was that to enjoy, and the warmth of his hand. Human contact, non-professional human contact. Felt good. It'd be nice to think that she'd be responding this way to any attractive man taking her hand right now—not just Wolfe—but Angel knew how her luck worked. Against her. It was him. It was this crush that had maybe become more. She'd lusted after him before even knowing him, but all this—especially knowing that he disliked Christmas but still did all this for the kids? Controlling her reaction was hopeless.

Of course, he would be even better than he'd seemed. Of. Course.

He led through a short alcove that functioned

as a hallway, and housed what she could only consider a reading nook with comfy chair, lamp and table, through the corner of the sanctuary, which she wasn't ready to see, to a proper hallway and a big, bright, white kitchen full of marble countertops, stainless-steel appliances—really big ones—and a tall beautiful window with yet another pointy arch on top. Church windows. Clear glass, not stained. Less valuable, her mind supplied. Less scary.

"See? It's not riddled with breakables. They're all stashed away in cupboards." He steered her over to a massive island in the center, spun her and picked her up to put her right on the counter. The concern she'd spied in his eyes earlier had entirely diminished when he'd begun teasing her in the stairwell, and now they practically blazed with mischief.

The twinkle in his eyes acted like a filter, only allowing new, attention-claiming emotions into her mind, and shoving that anxiety to the background.

"What?"

He stayed there with her so that her legs naturally parted to keep from putting any pressure on her knee stitches. He was right there, hips at the insides of her knees, and a little higher, his hands, large and warm, cupped the outside of each thigh and slid up, up, up, narrowing her whole world down to just this heartbeat, just this breath. But the eye contact the man gave, there was no breaking away from that.

"I could give you something else to worry about, make you less nervous about the household breakables."

"I thought you had a code."

"Found a loophole," he said, leaning in, his hands forming to her hips, then squeezing and sliding up. Waist. Ribs.

"What is it?" Was there any voice there, or was that all breath?

"We're not at work." He smiled, melting away all desire to ask further questions.

His hand on her jaw, long fingers cupping behind her head, he leaned in and she leaned in too.

"Been thinking about this since yesterday. Or longer."

He caught her upper lip between his, then just pressed tingling warmth into her. It was like a ravenous kiss that got distracted and stilled to soak in the sparkling tide of sensation that rolled out from it. Slow and savoring, with soft surprised noises from one—or both—of them.

The man kissed as if he had all the time in the world, and she were some rare, exotic wine to savor. To roll around on his tongue, to breathe in.

Whatever else he was, whatever else she lacked, didn't matter. It would end, she was leaving, going far enough away consequences couldn't follow.

She clutched at his shoulders, because her own spine seemed to be melting and she could end up a puddle on his fancy counter without an anchor. Finding some inner well of courage, or complete loss of sense, she pulled him closer and deepened the kiss.

When she slipped her tongue into his mouth, he gave up all semblance of control. The world tilted, and she couldn't tell which way was up, then he had her on her back, stretched out on the cold, pristine countertop, and he stretched out with her, kisses too hungry for artistry.

With the counter for a bed, he cradled her head on one arm, his other threading into her hair, hot ragged breaths filling the cool kitchen air, bouncing off the marble—needy, desperate echoes.

She became aware of some bells sounding in her head when he backed off enough to brace his forehead against hers. "You're ringing."

"I'm ringing?"

"Please tell me it's not recording us again." His breathless words identified the ringing. Not in her head, on her phone. In her pocket.

She had to force her fingers to uncurl from the fabric of his formerly smooth button-down, and she leaned to fish the phone out of her back pocket. "It's an alarm to get started. Not recording. We're supposed to start in five minutes."

"Five minutes," he repeated, and then caught her cheeks again for a much gentler few kisses. "You know I'm not done, right?"

"You're not done," she echoed, acutely aware of how relieved she sounded, then sighed. "Goodness, I'm just repeating everything you say."

"But do you feel better about the house?"

She hadn't even thought about the house, but his question forced her to do so as they sat up and the room stopped spinning. "At least the kitchen." Then, "We should unpack the cookies and icings and candies…"

"And the instructions?"

"Those too."

He climbed down and extended one hand like a gentleman to help her down, but his eyes still screamed scoundrel.

This wasn't over.

CHAPTER NINE

WOLFE FINISHED THE morning's surgery and made it through lunch without seeing Angel, but not without thinking about her. A busy schedule could save him from physically running into her, for a while, but nothing could keep his mind entirely focused. She'd even slipped in there during surgery, which was a sacred time, when he wanted his attention so razor sharp as to border on supernatural.

That was the goal, and that had not happened today. The reason he'd been hiding the last hour, eating his lunch in an empty office, was the hope he could get his head together and go five minutes without someone asking if they were dating, if they were going to the winter ball together.

He looked at his watch, scrubbed his hands over his face and headed for the door. He was supposed to meet her at one to get ready; no more avoiding the locker room where they were supposed to change into the ugly jumpers.

The entire point of last evening's shenanigans had been to build gingerbread houses to set up this afternoon's activity—eating gingerbread men and making their own with construction paper and cotton balls in the children's ward activities room.

That kiss had ruined him. He couldn't even pretend he could keep his head straight about her now. Not until this madness ran its course, and until she left town.

The thought caused his stomach to sour, and he retreated instinctively into the thousandth replay of that kiss.

He'd been sure he wouldn't break his rules. Not two minutes before she'd arrived, he'd been giving himself another stern lecture about keeping his hands to himself. Remembering the looks and comments he'd received from peers about them, not really about the shenanigans, and the spark that pulsed between them all the time. No one missed it. Except maybe the kids. He wasn't sure about Jenna. After the demand for a mistletoe kiss, she'd retreated into telling him he looked happy, and then casually mentioning Angel looked happy too. Really smooth.

As if he'd gotten amnesia over her asking him twice already to marry Angel so she wouldn't leave town.

Marry Dr. Angel—as if he could even picture that. Every time he tried to think of marriage, he got a mental image of his parents shrieking at one another, and occasionally throwing breakables.

He should've told Angel that one. He didn't keep breakables because they made him nervous, not that they'd be broken by accident, but that they'd end up as projectile weaponry.

Not that he could picture her doing that either. It would probably be him: *You are what you eat. You become what you know.* And none of that stopped him wanting her. Or liking her. He even worried about her, which was actually pretty annoying.

He'd been so confident in his self-control. Then she'd arrived, looking as white as that vat of frosting they'd eventually dove into, and all thoughts about a normal, run-of-the-mill cookie-construction campaign had fallen right out of his head. He'd kissed her. Then lost his damn mind.

Instead of a couple of hours together, five had flown by. That had also been his fault. More than half of that time had been them cleaning up the kitchen after the gingerbread death match he'd impulsively started after she'd handed him a frosting bag with a tiny spout, and he'd been unable to resist using the thing like a ropey, ineffective squirt gun. To make her smile again. Distracting her put her at ease, even if her reaction to his home was strange.

Comments on the stream and in person today had assured him the kids thought it was great. But by the end, they'd both been covered in frosting, buckets of crumbs and candy sprinkles. She'd been unable to leave without a shower. He'd literally locked himself in another bathroom, and every door between them, to keep from helping himself to her shower just so he could wash her sugar-frosted skin or give himself diabetes by licking her clean.

He pushed into the locker room. With any luck, someone else would be in there. Anyone. A buffer. Even Reynolds. God, especially Reynolds. She'd suck the temptation right out of the whole situation.

But he was alone, the jumper nowhere in sight.

Maybe she'd already changed and gone looking for him; he was a few minutes late. Maybe there was still hope.

He sat and braced his elbows on his knees,

stretching his shoulders forward to try and ease the tension that had his neck cracking every time he looked too far to the right.

A few minutes later, the squeaky door opened, and he heard her before she rounded the locker bank. He knew it was her by the cadence of her steps, and if that wasn't some sign he was in trouble, he didn't know what could be.

"You all right?" she asked, stopping beside him so that he had a good view of her shoes, and laid a gentle hand on his shoulder.

"Tough surgery," he lied, then lifted his head. "Stiff shoulders."

That was true at least.

Her hand stayed there, and she looked at him so seriously he almost fell for it. "Is this a war injury?"

"War?"

"Last night. There were no memory-corrupting head injuries I'm aware of." Teasing. Flirting. Perfection. "I suspect it's more from the clean-up than the actual battle. Big baby."

He felt his smile start in his chest, and he was chuckling by the time it got to his mouth. "I told you the cleaning people would take care of it today, but no."

"That's right. I clean up my own messes. Not spoilt like some Scottish cookie war losers."

"You have to stop saying Scottish. I'm not *ish*. I'm a Scotsman. I'm a Scot. Not *ish*. *Ish* is when somethin' is a bit like somethin' else. I'm a Scot, and if you start doubtin' me I'll be in here in a kilt tomorrow, and then you'll have to defend my virtue from all the ravenous women in this hospital." He stood up, unable to remember why he'd dreaded seeing her when it actually felt so good. Especially now that she was playing with him in return, it wasn't just him lobbing teases to be met by her huge-eyed blinks.

"You think women would?" she asked, then just shook her head. "Never mind. You're right. You have too many women wrapped around your little finger without doing anything so blatantly sexy."

"To American women."

"To all women!"

"American-ish women."

She laughed in return and opened her locker to retrieve a red and green jumper, which she handed to him.

"Green, eh?"

"I didn't invent the Christmas colors," she

said, then pulled out another garish jumper for herself. "Look at the front."

She held hers to her chest, and he had to fight to not just think about the curves the jumper draped over. Reindeer. Gargantuan head. Little red bulb at the nose.

His would be Santa; he knew without even opening it.

"Right, let's do this, then," he said, turning his back to her so that he could maintain some level of decency while she changed.

That was the intention at least.

She went along with his direction, and though he'd been hoping she'd find a bathroom to change in, the sound of rustling cotton told him it was happening there, behind him.

He grabbed trousers from his locker and kicked his shoes off, trying to get done as quickly as he could.

Only his balance was all messed up from his attention riveted to the sound of her undressing at his back.

Locker rooms aren't sexy.

He repeated twice to himself to keep from turning around despite being so desperate to look that his imagination provided visuals anyway.

The freckles. He knew they'd be on her back,

chest, maybe lower. He hoped lower. Anywhere sun had touched, he might find them, and though he doubted that Angel was the type to ever go nude sunbathing, there might be freckled, permanent tan lines on the cheeks of her bum. Wouldn't that be something?

He wobbled and sat down before he fell on his face trying to get out of his scrub bottoms, cracking his shoulder loudly on the locker door on the way down.

"You okay?"

"Just bumped the door," he muttered, tugging off the other shoe so that he could get the scrub bottoms off. Smooth. No game. No game at all today.

She wasn't clanging around like a drunk or looking away. Her gaze on his back felt almost as physical as her hand on his shoulder moments ago.

Standing again, he threw the bottoms down, then stepped into the trousers, trying to be so quiet. Trying to listen to her, not just because he was suddenly a creepy jerk who got turned on by the sound of a woman dressing, but because he wanted to know when she was done. When he could safely stop averting his eyes.

But in the effort to listen to her, all he heard was his heartbeat, and his ragged breaths.

Maybe he was the one who should've gone to the dammed bathroom to change.

"You sure you're okay?"

"I'm fine." He fastened the trousers, then looked into the locker, no longer sure what the next step was in dressing. "Am I supposed to wear something beneath this?"

"Like a turtleneck?" she asked, and he nodded, staring hard into his locker.

"I don't have one."

"I didn't bring one either. I hate them."

"Me too," he murmured. "I have a tee shirt, or the scrub top."

"It's an acrylic fiber, not wool, you could wear it without anything under and not suffer, but a tee shirt is fine."

And he was taking forever. He grabbed the tee shirt and yanked it over his head.

"I'm just going to wear this beneath mine."

Without conscious thought, he turned to look and found her holding up a long-sleeved undershirt, often layered beneath scrubs for warmth. But she wasn't wearing it right now.

Bottoms. Pink cotton bra. And freckles. Good God, the freckles. Over her chest, the swells of her breasts, so close in color to the otherwise sensible bra.

Belly too, his gaze kept traveling down. Less thick there, but present. On her hips. Her trousers sat low enough to see that curve that had bewitched him on the way to the tree lighting, and it was exactly as he'd convinced himself it wasn't.

"Wolfe?"

He was doing it again.

"This is a hot mess, Angel," he muttered, dragging his gaze to the ceiling and licking his suddenly dry lips. "My willpower is extremely brittle right now."

She took the suggestion and shook the top out to shimmy into it.

"I'm sorry, I was… That was very…not how I usually operate. Not operate. I don't operate. Like surgery. I hated surgical rotations." She seemed to realize she was babbling and puffed out a slow breath. "I meant with men. I'm not good with men, and that. Flirting, I guess."

"That was you trying to flirt?" He looked at her again and breathed a little easier to find her skin all covered up.

"I was trying to see if you still thought I'd be fun to kiss after you kissed me last night," she explained, in the most ridiculous and adorable manner, her hands gesturing in this weird dismissive wave, as if she were stuck between fanning herself and shooing herself away.

Not confident, though he couldn't imagine why.

Before he'd thought it through, he stepped right over the bench separating them and grabbed her cheeks, then pressed his mouth to hers. Kept pressing until the lockers were at her back and she was grabbing at his hips, his waist, around and under his shirt, pulling him closer, seeking skin.

Deeper than last night's kiss, he stroked his tongue into her mouth, and the world tilted when she moaned low enough to rumble his lips and tongue.

Need and want sparked through him, obliterating his self-control and all desire to participate in today's shenanigans unless they were private, and in his bedroom.

Boldly, despite her moment of doubt, her hands slid under his shirt, contouring the muscles of his bare back, and the feel of her soft hands on his skin rippled out and his imagination took over. It was just his back, but it might as well have been a direct touch to his front, because that was where it all converged.

When his body began to ready, harden, he broke from the kiss, but still couldn't break entirely away from her. His mind demanded it, but still he licked and sucked down her neck, causing the most delightful stuttering gasp to wrench out of her.

It echoed.

His heart beat hard enough to pulse in his vision, and even his harsh breathing echoed, and a metallic creak.

The locker behind her.

Because…they were in the locker room.

Damn.

"I want you," he panted against her neck, then leaned back, done fighting it. All he could bear was to postpone. This couldn't happen there. They had the kids to think of, and if he was going to throw his personal code down the toilet, he'd do it right. At home. "Come to my house."

"For the tree?"

She looked as dazed as he felt, and her lips were so pink he found himself thinking of the color of flesh he'd find lower. Would it match her lips? Her nipples?

"No."

He should put some air between them, but his body ignored his orders. He just stayed mashed against her, even knowing she'd feel how hard he'd grown. What she did to him.

"Why?"

"I need help movin' furniture." He couldn't help playing with her, eyes locked to her heated, hungry gaze, and added thickly, "The bed, specifically."

"The bed," she repeated, and nodded, as if she didn't have to think about it at all. "Okay."

"Okay." He repeated her this time, because it had somehow become insanely sexy that she couldn't string together a sentence right now.

"For sex," she suddenly blurted out.

And here he thought he was being direct.

"Yes. Lots of loud, obnoxious sex. Messy, filthy, moderately untidy...whatever." He said those things partly to see if he could make her blush hotter—and he did—but then realized she needed the reassurance of actual words and added, "With me. Since you seem to want to spell things out."

"Okay."

Okay?

He couldn't stop the grin now if he tried. "How's your knee?"

"Okay?"

"Good." He stepped back, pulling himself from her and sitting directly down in the hopes his galloping heart slowed. "I need a minute before we go up."

"Okay."

Fourth time that word had come out in a row. He looked at her, still leaning on the locker, expression as scrambled as his brain.

"Are you all right?"

The question seemed to get her moving again. Her nod jerky and uncoordinated enough to suggest a neck injury. "Need to finish and, er, get upstairs."

Yes, they did. They had that whole gingerbread thing.

Then he was dragging her home with him. Directly home, to spend the night.

Nothing should have been less sexy than spending time with sixteen sticky-fingered children making gingerbread people for the bulletin board, but every time she watched him crouch down to help a child with a fussy bit of cotton, or fetch a dropped crayon, she saw him as a daddy. A real dad. A good dad. The kind who did arts and crafts with his children and made airplane sounds while zooming a cookie toward a crooked little smile. The effect was hell on her stability.

Wonderful to behold, but not exactly sexy until it led to picturing just how those imaginary children would be made. Not the whole time, but it popped up now and then, and every time it brought some strange trembling in her torso. Infuriating and persistent. An earthquake only she could feel. Impossible to ignore, but light enough she could *almost* function.

Until he looked at her. When he looked at her, when his startlingly pale blue eyes locked to hers across the room, the rumble went from low-grade aftershocks to the kind of tremor that could shake and crumble foundations.

Now, as the last of the children were escorted back to their rooms, Wolfe caught her tidying up scraps of paper. "We're done."

"We made a mess."

He wasn't shaking; nothing about this rattled him in the slightest. He'd said his willpower was brittle, but if he touched her and felt the tremble, he might actually drag her to the ER.

"I'm going. You're going too." He looked at her mouth, but, after a couple of slow blinks, pulled back and turned to lead her out. Still holding her hand, dragging her behind him.

He didn't stop until they were in a cab, and only waited until it was outside easy eyeshot of the hospital before pulling her to him and launching right back into the kiss they'd aborted for cookie time.

CHAPTER TEN

BY THE TIME they'd made the short drive to Tribeca, Angel had forgotten entirely about the driver. She knew only one thing: *him*. The way he smelled. The rasp of his stubble on her skin. The glide of his tongue. His fingers stroking her jaw, her neck, tangling in her hair. The heady pleasure of being so wanted.

She'd never had that. Sex, infrequent even before she'd moved to the city where she'd never feel at home, had only ever been *nice*.

They weren't near a bed, fully dressed, and just *kissing*, but it seared into her in a way she couldn't ignore. In a way that would leave a hole when it ended, and feeling that, knowing that, she still couldn't hold part of herself back.

All she could do was hope that he gave back whatever his kisses demanded later or leaving would be harder.

Even if his interest evaporated, right now she felt like the focus of his world too, and it sang through her in a way that made it possible to let go. In Wolfe's arms, she was sexier, stronger, *enough*. At least for now.

It took the driver announcing they'd arrived for either of them to notice. Wolfe tossed some money through the partition, and they ran to his door. His church-house door. Her courage faltered for a second. Holding hands with this man and running toward a church wasn't prophetic, no matter what popped into her mind after an afternoon picturing him as a dad. It was impossible, no matter that hope-drenched lifting in her chest.

Once inside, he twirled her to press against the fancy, pointed door, laying another drugging kiss on her already addled senses. A lock clicked, and they were moving again.

In a long, stumbling kiss, they made it to the stairwell she'd nearly traversed last night and up about three steps. Her foot caught, she only didn't fall down the stairs because his arms firmed, and he steered them to the nearby wall, to hit and slide down.

"Kissing and climbing stairs is outside your skill set, Dr. Angel." He laughed against her lips, his voice full of the soft, warm amusement she couldn't process. He was laughing at them both, and teasing in a way that didn't feel pointed, or derogatory. Another thing she found so attractive about him. The whole time she'd known Wolfe, she'd never heard him say something harsh or judgmental about anyone aside from his parents. *She'd* made fun of her attending's name, but he hadn't joined in. She was the worst person of them, as if she needed proof.

The thoughts turned her hands clumsier, and when trying to wrestle him out of his sweater she managed to scratch his side.

The sound he made wasn't so much intended to make her stop—he certainly wasn't stopping. In fact just after he grunted from the clumsy, fumbled caress, he redoubled his efforts to kiss her senseless, and make her clumsier.

No reprimand came. No making fun of her unartful seduction.

He laughed again. He was just happy, or this was *fun* to him—not malicious as she'd grown to expect to hear from people. It was warm, as if he even found her gracelessness endearing.

She grabbed his head and nipped at his upper lip until they were both stretched out on the stairs. Not long, he wrapped his arms around her middle and rolled so she straddled his lap and the carpeted angles pressed into his back, not hers.

As soon as she put the slightest pressure on her knee, she cried out into his mouth and leveraged back off. All the way off. Until she was standing.

"Oh, darlin', I forgot your knee. Let me see."

"I forgot too," she panted, both from the shock of pain and from all the oxygen deprivation of the past half an hour.

But he still ushered her up the stairs to the landing, reached for the button of her trousers and unfastened them.

The heavy black material fell loud even against the thick carpet, and he went down with it. On his knees before her, he eyed the bandage, tilting his head as he prodded lightly, no doubt looking for signs of bleeding or increased pain.

"It's feeling better. It was just a little burning reminder." The pain passed, and she didn't mind it anymore. She wanted more of him. If she was going to end up broken and bloody at the bottom of this canyon she was sure she'd spent a lifetime scrambling up, she was going to throw herself over the edge to give the best view on the way down as she fell for him.

Falling. The plummeting in her middle happened whenever she was around him, and only eased with his touch.

But he stayed kneeling, then guided her hands to his shoulders so he could get her shoes off, and continue undressing her.

"Turn around," he said, his voice thick and rasping with such emotion she could do nothing but obey.

Without the cloth around her ankles, she even managed it without falling.

He didn't say another word, just hooked his fingers in her panties and pulled them straight down.

The shock of the suddenness left her speechless. She knew what they were up to, and she'd signed up for it—she'd have signed a waiver if he'd asked—but still, he'd gone from gentle and caring to ass-baring in a heartbeat and whatever self-control she had shattered.

And then, when she couldn't stand it anymore, she felt the first brush of his fingers along the swell of each cheek, stroking a matching arch from her hips, down to the underside of each cheek, ending between her legs.

The shaking in her torso returned, now more of a quiver low in her belly. "Wolfe."

Her voice sounded strangled and desperate even to her own ears, but he didn't answer.

Not with words. There was some sound, but he kept up, thumbs pressing and stroking, molding her flesh so that cool air hit parts of her body usually hidden, making clear how exposed she was to his eye-level view. The acute vulnerability summoned her voice again.

"Wolfe?"

It was just his name, and as hoarse as she'd ever heard herself sound. Tense. And *excited*.

In answer, he gently gripped her hips and turned her back to him. Still there before her, but not for long. He rose long enough to claim another kiss, and another, and soon they were halfway up that second flight of stairs, staggering, stumbling and pawing at one another.

She managed to get his insane sweater off, and threw it over her head, lights still twinkling somewhere.

He helped her out of hers, then her bra, and it was as if the man were all hands and eyes. He couldn't see enough, couldn't touch enough, and what had started as fun had suddenly become so intense neither of them smiled or laughed anymore.

They'd reached the top, she realized when she

reached back to climb and found only flat floor behind her. It was then that he broke from kissing her, naked but for socks, and kissed his way down between her legs.

Whatever she'd thought sex with Wolfe Mc-Keag would be like, it wasn't this. He had no hesitation about anything. He wanted to see, he stripped her down. He wanted to taste her, he parted her legs. He made her his, at least for that moment. Without words, without promises, she was his, and he accepted her. Every part of her. Every part he could uncover and lay his brand on.

The consuming pleasure of his wicked mouth and talented tongue had her almost sobbing with the pleasure cleaving through her far too soon, and that plummeting sensation surged into every inch of her, every cell.

He didn't stop until he'd wrung every shuddering second of her orgasm from her, and then he was up and lifting her.

Wordless, thoughtless, she knew he was carrying her somewhere—probably the bed—but could only hold on. Letting him carry her, without questioning her safety, certain in him.

Trusting. Without hesitation, the thought swam up. Had that ever happened before?

No. The answer rang through her before the question had even fully formed. Not that she could remember. Not even as a child, when she'd felt insecure in everything, even in being carried by her parents—she'd held on tight.

Not even when she'd told Spencer about her past, and how she'd ended up incarcerated for her family. In the back of her mind, she'd been braced for rejection. So well trained to it, when it had come it hadn't hurt half as much as she'd expected. Just confirmed what a lifetime being tied to her family had taught: the only person she could count on was her. The only one who would be so concerned about her being hurt.

But she trusted *Wolfe*. She only held on to get *closer* to him.

"Don't stiffen up," he said, rounding a corner in the hall and heading through double doors into a long, dimly lit room.

"I'm not."

"You are," he said, voice gruff but gentle. "I won't drop you."

"I know," she said, because she did, down to her bones. And that was the scary part. How dumb was it to trust so implicitly when there had been no promises between them? Nothing but an unspoken understanding that whatever happened between them had a predetermined expiration date.

When they entered the space, a sense of comfort nipped at her, something she hadn't felt in his massive, beautiful kitchen or the marble-columned living room.

It was only New York dark inside, but the darkness had color.

He turned to navigate furniture, and she finally saw the source of light. The massive rose window he'd spoken of. It took up the whole wall in the narrow, vaulted room, and the lights of the city glowing beyond sent pinks and blues cascading through.

"You like it. I knew you would." He sounded genuinely pleased as he eased her onto the bed haloed in the ethereal glow, and crawled over her, the evidence of his need still jutting boldly from his body.

She didn't want to talk about the window. If her knee could stand it, she'd guide him to his back and regain some control. Because being on top was safer. Because she'd be responsible for her own happiness and satisfaction. Because she wanted to give the same sensation to him, so she wasn't the only one falling into the canyon.

But she couldn't. He plucked a condom from

the nightstand and the heat and weight of him settled between her legs.

She grabbed his cheeks and pulled his beautiful mouth back to hers. All she could do was pour it into her kiss, into her touch, and pray he felt it too.

This kind of trust couldn't come without love. She loved him and now had no idea how she could leave or if she even wanted to anymore. If she could keep this, keep *him*, after Christmas, she'd stay.

Wolfe was never good at recognizing shifts in a relationship, which was a big part of why his relationship attempts always failed. Until the shift became seismic and the ground actually moved, he didn't see it. Even the times he'd recognized the stresses building up, he'd never been able to release them without causing destruction.

Lying there with Angel, his head resting on her belly and body angled to keep all pressure away from her knee, he knew the ground was shifting. He just didn't know what it meant.

The slow in and out of her breathing created a relaxing cadence beneath his cheek, and her arm across his shoulders was gentle, tender even, but it was there, buzzing beneath them.

They'd just made the ground move and now neither of them said a word.

His bag of tricks had one basic trick in it: levity. He could try to make her laugh, but that would diminish whatever had just happened.

"Are you asleep?" she whispered, considerate, and sweet, not someone prone to joking around to dispel other emotions she didn't know how to deal with.

"No."

He didn't know what else to say. Or feel. Or think.

"You want me to go now?"

The simple question, so softly spoken, still shot cold through the back of his neck. He lifted from the bed to look at her, to see what the quiet words didn't tell him—why she'd asked him that.

He saw the answer, written in the uneven pinch of her brows. Uncertainty tinged with fear.

If she thought he didn't want dates staying around, he couldn't really fault her for thinking that. But the *now* made it feel pointed. As if he'd gotten what he wanted and was done with her. Like a word used to *discard* her.

"Why would you think that?" he asked, unable to keep irritation out of his voice.

Her eyes shifted to the side and the shrug she gave him washed away his desire to do or say the right thing. He was just going to ask what he needed to ask.

"Are you still judging me by Lyons? I know he was a jerk to you in some manner—that's just who he is now—but you tell me exactly what I did that made you leap to that insulting conclusion."

Somewhere in that, his irritation had tipped straight over into anger. Not his intention, but there it was—the best sex of his life came with the most puzzling woman.

"No." She raised onto her elbows, maybe readying to leave, but her answer didn't clear anything up.

"No which?"

"Not Lyons…"

"So, I did something."

"No," she repeated, then looked so chastised he took a breath before trying again.

"Just tell me what he did. You know I'm worried about him—maybe it'd help me understand how to help him if I knew more."

Underhanded, maybe. Playing on her sympathies for sure. And still true.

Her blue eyes shone blue-black like a raven's

wing in the low light cast through the rose window, which she'd now focused on rather than him.

If it weren't for the consideration he saw on her face, he'd have been on his feet, calling a cab for her to go. She was thinking about it, but the fact that she even needed to spoke to how much it had affected her. Even if he hadn't seen it in her face a dozen times over the past few days, he'd know it now.

"He thinks I'm a stupid hillbilly," she said finally and didn't so much as glance at him. Her eyes were so locked to the window, wider than usual, waiting, her whole body stiff.

Once upon a time, his brother had been charming. Just not for the last year or so, and it still had the ability to shock Wolfe.

"He said that?" he asked. "Why?"

Her wide eyes dimmed a bit and she half shrugged. "He implied it."

"What did he say?"

"He had a patient with a thick accent, and he called on me to translate because she sounded just like me only more incomprehensible."

Not the worst thing he'd even heard Lyons say *this week*, but pretty pointed for someone he wasn't actively quarreling with. "Had something happened?"

She shook her head, and then finally did look at him, worry he'd seen on her face softening just a little. Trusting a little more, but still uncertain. "He just came to get me."

"And said this incomprehensible hillbilly sounds dumb, you talk to her?"

"He said he couldn't understand a word, that he wanted me to go talk to her. I asked why, and he said, 'Because she sounds like she just fell off a mountaintop in Tennessee. Like you, only worse.'"

More incomprehensible than Angel, who wasn't incomprehensible, but he still didn't hear the word *stupid* in there, though that was how she'd taken it.

"Did you tell him it was Georgia? Do they have mountains in Georgia?"

"The Appalachians start in Georgia."

"Was that the mountain you fell off?"

He tried to joke, because that was the only good tactic in his bag of tricks, but she frowned harder. "I'm not from Georgia."

"Tennessee?"

"No." Her shoulders had grown rigid; his own started to ache in sympathy.

She was evasive about where she was from. Anyone else would've said, *No, I'm from X.*

Later. He'd ask where later.

"Still not hearing stupid, love. You think his request means a judgment of her capabilities?"

She snorted then pulled away, moving to rise. "Course it does. He judged her stupid because of her background and the way she talks. It's a common thing. People do it all the time."

Judgment. This was about judgment. The reason she kept to herself, all of it.

"What else happened? Who else?"

She paused and rubbed both her hands over her face, now standing beside the bed. "Listen, I know you think this is meaningless talk, but it's not to me. It's not easy to talk about some things. Sometimes you have something, or things that happened, and then you just have to try and forget and move on."

Seismic shift. Wolfe rose from the bed with far greater care, certain even the slightest wrong move would send this spiraling out of his control. But he had to know. "What else happened?"

"You want a list?" She almost laughed, her voice rising, nearly shouting. "How far back should I go? You want to hear about the little old lady at church who tried to wash my freckles off because she just assumed I was dirty?"

He didn't even know how to process that question, or the anger. But he understood finally what so unnerved her about the house and made her keep to herself.

"Sweetheart, you have to let these things go. Things happen, I get it, and they change you. But who you are is pretty great. Maybe you wouldn't be so kind to everyone if these bad things hadn't happened to you." There, that sounded right to him.

"So, Lyons should just get over being shot? I doubt that'll make him feel better." She started walking to the stairs with a subject change. She didn't want to talk about herself. "Probably already thinkin' that to hisself anyway. You think I don't think that way? Just get over it. Just get over this, and that, and all them other things. And I'm tryin', but I gotta stop makin' the same mistakes. If Lyons is gonna get better, he has to do it hisself. It's good you wanna be there for him, but you can't force folks to feel *this* just 'cause you think it's silly to feel *that*."

Or not the right thing to say. He followed, mentally scrambling for the right thing. She was after her clothes, and all that was on the stairs.

"You don't know what it is like to live with that. You don't know what it's like to be *him*, so you can't fix him. You might get it was *really bad* bein' almost murdered, but you can't know how it changed the way he sees hisself or the world. And it had ta change him. Big things, sometimes even things that seem small to others, if they happen enough, they leave a mark."

Definitely not about Lyons. She was compassionate, but she swapped back and forth between talking about Lyons and herself. And the accent. Goodness, the accent got thicker and thicker. She wasn't shouting now, but her voice wobbled, and she might have sniffed. Like at the rink when she'd fallen and wanted to show the kids that it was important to keep getting back up. Because of all the times she'd had to make herself get back up. He knew without her saying.

"Are you leaving New York because of Lyons?"

"I'm leaving because of *all* the Lyonses." She picked up garments on the way down the stairs.

"Hey." He didn't want her to go. And he really didn't want her to go on these terms. "Stop. Just wait."

"I need to go home. I'm workin' tomorrow."

"I know, I'm working tomorrow too." He

caught her around the waist when she reached the landing and found her panties. "You can stay. I can get you home early enough to change. You're upset. I don't know what just happened. I didn't mean to hurt you."

But he was notorious for it. And despite all his talk about this being all right because it wasn't a real relationship, he'd fallen right back into that pattern where as soon as he tried to get serious about something, about anything, he hurt the one he was with. As soon as he stopped trying to make people laugh, someone got hurt. Which should inform his decision about Lyons. Maybe she was right, and he should let his brother work things out on his own. But she obviously wasn't working things out on her own. She was running.

"I hate gettin' up that early," she muttered, but didn't pull away from him.

He wrapped his arms around her until they were locked together, back to front, and he could rest his chin on her shoulder. "I'm sorry I brought up something painful, Angel. I didn't even get a chance to ask you to the winter ball on Saturday before I messed it up."

Her head drooped forward, and she shook it

in a display of weariness that made him want to carry her right back upstairs.

"I don't know if we should go together."

It was a mess, and exactly the wrong time to push. "Let me drive you home."

She shook her head, then disengaged his arms from her waist so she could step into the panties he'd peeled off her. The panties that fit perfectly along the freckled proof she'd tanned in a bikini a few times in her life.

She stepped into her trousers and shook her head. "No reason for both of us to go out in the cold, but you can call me a cab."

He had to remind himself he'd said he wasn't going to push her tonight—*twice*—before he was able to nod and retrieve his own trousers and the phone he'd abandoned in shedding them.

Tomorrow, after this had calmed down, he'd talk to her again.

Or maybe it was time to speak with his brother about Angel, since it was just about as easy to get information about Angel from Angel as it was to get information from Lyons about Lyons. But she had talked about his brother when pressed and revealed a little more about herself along the way.

Manipulative—a trait he hadn't picked up

from his mother, but now wished he had. Maybe Lyons would talk about Angel and reveal something Wolfe could use to help him too. Maybe it would even help their beleaguered relationship to speak about something *else*.

He generally blindly stumbled a route through the blasted landscape of human emotions. No maps here. No real landmarks. Malfunctioning compass. Following this one light on the horizon was all he had, when everything was starting to feel *important*.

CHAPTER ELEVEN

LATE THE NEXT AFTERNOON, after a day stuck in a cycle of questioning herself and her decisions, Angel stepped out of the treatment room where she'd just treated a copper-curled toddler who'd discovered a bead would fit wonderfully far up her nose, and hadn't made it ten paces when the sound of two male Scottish voices stopped her dead in the hallway.

Wolfe talking with Lyons. She could identify the sound of his voice, but not the words. She could also hear the strain, which was why she took another couple of steps closer. They were kind of, almost dating. If he was in distress, shouldn't she help?

"She's using you, don't you get that?" Lyons said, not exactly shouting, but even with the door half closed, she would've understood every word without purposefully eavesdropping, which she really shouldn't be doing…

The thought drifted off when Lyons's words

actually processed. When they did, something cold enveloped her, as surely as if she'd just fallen through ice.

Lyons hadn't said her name, but he was talking to Wolfe. This was about *her*. She was the one being accused of *using* him. She looked quickly down the hall and back, making sure no one else had come down the small, far-off hallway while her attention had been focused elsewhere. It was bad enough that she and Wolfe had already become part of the hospital gossip mill without Lyons making matters worse by throwing around such accusations. Any Sutcliffe employee would know he'd meant her.

Swallowing down the acid rising in her throat took almost superhuman strength. She should stop listening; it wouldn't be making her guts churn if she'd kept on walking. But then she couldn't keep someone else from hearing either—as if she could now. No, they'd just see her lurking and have a *real* story to tell, not just some more of Lyons's rantings to dismiss.

Angel looked back the way she'd come, considering a different route to where she needed to go. If she took the stairs, she could go up to the next floor and down three hallways to the elevators, and then come back down. Then she wouldn't have to stand here, where she might throw up, and she wouldn't have to risk Wolfe seeing her, and knowing she'd overheard them fighting about her. Not that she could hear anything except urgent-sounding utterings now. Maybe they were wrapping it up. She should go before they came out and found her there.

What possible reason could they even have to do this at work? She understood emotions running high and losing control, but Wolfe had told her how he hated workplace drama. It was why he didn't usually date at work. If they were dating, which she wasn't sure about. Did Lyons just not care about scandal?

"She's not innocent, no matter what her name is."

Lyons.

Was Wolfe defending her? If he was, it was quieter.

When was the last time someone had defended her? The thought almost brought a smile to her face and that lifting in her chest again. Hope stayed her feet. The hope that he felt this thing between them too. Maybe she *could*.

"I can't protect you forever. Someday you'll

have to grow up and see how the world works. How people truly are. Just ask her what she wants from you." Lyons.

"She doesn't want anything. She doesn't even matter."

Wolfe.

That one was Wolfe, his voice finally rising enough for her to make out the words, and it was to shout about how little she meant to him? Her stomach lurched in a way the toddler's bloody snot had failed to elicit.

She'd known this would be short-term, having planned her move for a while, but last night had confused her. Made her want to change her plans. She even knew that Wolfe considered her an easy relationship to have because of the fact she was leaving, and there'd be nothing to tie him down in a couple more weeks. That had been before last night. Even if she'd panicked and fled, it hadn't been because she regretted them being together. She'd run because she'd felt...*too much.* And a little freaked out by that. But now hearing him shout that she meant nothing?

It took a couple of good swallows, ignoring the way her heart suddenly seemed out of rhythm and the light-headed sensation that came with it, for Angel to start moving again, back the way she'd come from to find those stairs.

It was going to be bad enough to feel the eyes of her coworkers on her as she tried to pretend nothing had happened without suffering his heavy gaze as well. How many of them would agree with Lyons's assessment of her character? Putting up walls was the only way she'd figured out how to get through. It had helped her survive the bullying that had come from being the poorest child in the school, and the daughter of a family of perpetually incarcerated petty criminals. Shut it all down, lock away the things she'd be judged for.

All she had to do was slow her heart rate down or start moving slowly enough to keep up with the oxygen supply that flutter pumped, sort out her patients' discharge—which should've already been done—attend her next patient and possibly steal a defibrillator for her handbag.

She had some time to calm down before she had to go to his church house and decorate the darned tree. Then find a way to be done with all this. She'd done enough.

He wouldn't care. She didn't matter anyway.

* * *

Everyone drank wine at the holidays. Or some kind of liquor. Beer. Cocktails. Moonshine. Angel was sure of it. And now that she'd been thrust into full-on participation in the joyousness, it was practically expected she imbibe.

Which was why she'd purchased three bottles of wine on her way home from work and had a small glass of each—to determine which she liked best—before calling the cab to take her to Wolfe's church house.

His church house of sin. Where things happened that didn't matter.

And when a girl got liquored up to go decorate a Christmas tree at a church house for the entertainment of ill children in the hospital, she wore her Sunday best. Including heels of some sort. The sort she'd selected were knee-high boots that both hid her knee bandage and went with the pretty white dress with winter blue flowers.

Now, standing outside Wolfe's front door, she couldn't think of a single thing except his loud statement. She couldn't seem to dismiss it, like that annoying jingle from that horrible toy commercial. Even the wine hadn't turned down the volume. It completely canceled out her admittedly spotty ability to think of anything entertaining to say, or even pretend there was some way to go back to that grand room without losing her mind.

To go where the window was—where he wanted to put the tree—meant she had to go where his bed was, where things happened that didn't matter!

It was a lot to ask.

He hadn't met her outside tonight, which should remind her exactly how low she rated. He'd been far more eager to see her prior to last night's nothing-important-that-happened.

It took nearly three minutes for Wolfe to make it to the door. She would've given up waiting and returned home if the cab hadn't left.

"Hi." He looked a bit disheveled, his dark hair mussed in the front as it had become when she'd plowed her hands through the thick, wavy locks last night. And he wasn't dressed up for this tree business, wearing a pair of jeans and a long-sleeved black V-necked sweater, showing off his broad shoulders, narrow waist and the tiniest bit of chest hair.

Very freaking sexy. Bastard. And it probably counted as dressed up just because he looked so good.

"I'm here to decorate, but I don't want to

talk about anything," she announced—almost shouted—emboldened by the wine that she'd drunk to kill her feelings. Or she was just using it as an excuse now that an hour or so had passed.

His perplexed blink only added coal to the boozy fire in her belly.

Whatever. She brushed past him to get inside and shed her coat and get this nightmare over with. Nightmares always happened after you lost your coat or fell in your heels.

He closed the door behind her, and then was there, helping her out of her coat like someone he cared about. "Everything all right?"

No.

And *no.*

Further, *no.*

And that wasn't concern for her. It was simply civilized host behavior. Which was why she didn't immediately recognize it—being a dumb hillbilly and all.

She got her arms out of the sleeves, put her handbag on the table there and stepped over to summon the elevator.

"You want to ride up?" He sounded so confused. Worried, her mind said, but that couldn't be it. Tension. It was tension.

"Yes."

There, she'd spoken.

But the wine? Hadn't helped a bit. It wasn't going to make the evening easier. Nothing could make this evening easier. "I don't want to go to the stairwell. I don't want to go to the room, but that's where the window is, unless you've decided to put it somewhere else."

He nodded slowly and, when the elevator door dinged, stepped inside and waited for her. "I already moved the bed out of the frame, set up the tripod and camera, and got the laptop booted for you to log in."

He didn't comment on her lack of desire for the stairs. Or the bed. Or any of it. He just held the door. As she stepped into the small metal box, her heel caught on the threshold, and she stumbled, catching herself on the frame as he reached out to steady her, that look on his face turning to alarm.

"Are you half-cut?"

"I don't know what that means," she whispered. Loudly. While giving him her most baleful stare.

No, this was not what the wine was supposed to do for her.

"Drunk," he filled in, his hands still out as if he was going to have to steady her even though her stumbling was more a fault of lazy walking than liquor.

"No." First answer. "Not anymore. Now I'm just kind of feeling sleepy. And...done." She puffed. "Let's just get this stupid thing over with, okay?"

"You're pissed, and you're pissed. Got it."

The doors closed.

He pushed the button, the only button, and it began to move.

It was only one floor. An especially tall floor, granted, but it couldn't take more than half a minute to get there. Half a minute wasn't so long when he wasn't reacting to her.

"You going to tell me why you're glaring daggers? Or am I to guess my brother did something again?"

Her eyes started rolling before he was half through the question.

"It was my department. You can't have thought I wouldn't..." She started to say *overhear*, the word was on her tongue, but why bother lying about this? "I was seeing a patient on the hall when you had your fight. I heard. So, let's just get this over with."

He reached for her arm and looked so sincere. It was even in his voice, sincere and a bit bewildered, as if he couldn't imagine what he'd have said that would make her cringe back from him. Or drive her to attempt an at-home wine-numbing session before she came over. "You know Lyons is an ass. We've talked about that."

Truth was, before he'd begun talking about how meaningless she was, she wouldn't have thought it would bother her. Only once she'd heard those words from his mouth, it had. The hurt and ache still rang through her, and she couldn't pretend not to understand why.

She'd progressed well past a crush. The time with him—while short—had lit something in her, had made her happy after a long stretch of loneliness and occasional misery. When you put that kind of physical attraction with emotional attraction, true feelings were bound to develop, she told herself. But it didn't help.

"Yes, we have," she agreed, then turned her arm so that his grip slipped off; the doors dinged and opened, and she stepped immediately out. "I don't want to talk anymore."

All she had to do was turn a corner and walk through the massive arched doors toward the rose window, and she could do that.

She heard him behind her, and the hair on her neck stood up from the weight of his stare, the proximity, the sensation he was going to grab her, and her own private hell of not knowing whether she'd let him. If she even had it in her to say *no* if he made a move. It was just too much to deal with in one day.

She stepped around the corner, and the double doors stood open, allowing her to focus on the silhouette of the tree framed by the rose window at the far end of the gallery-style room.

"Angel." He grabbed her elbow and stopped her, turning her toward him. "I went to talk to him to figure out if I could help somehow. It started on the wrong foot and went downhill from there."

"I heard." She pulled her elbow from his grasp and marched toward the tree. "Just turn on the dammed camera and let's get this over with. Where are the lights? It's supposed to start with lights."

He flipped on spotlights recessed in the ceiling to light the room up and she went to the laptop to login. The set of his jaw and his new glower said he at least felt *something* for her: anger.

"I'll get the fairy lights."

The quiet, even keel of his speech—lacking all his usual melody—said something else.

That she'd *wronged* him. He was somehow the wounded party. Wounded party! She could feel the scowl her features had settled into, the muscles of her forehead burned like calves on a long-distance run, but she couldn't get them to unclench.

All she could do was go to the tree for him to hand lights over so they could wind them around, but every time he touched her hand, it sent a jolt of anger through her the wine utterly failed to dampen. Or maybe the wine was just gone. She really didn't know, she didn't drink that frequently, and never with the purpose of self-medicating her way through a Christmas tree decorating.

"These lights are the multicolored kind," he said to the camera, talking to the kids since she refused to respond anytime he tried to talk to her, other than jerking her hand away as if he were a deranged lava monster anytime they touched.

He was narrating, but it wasn't in the vicinity of cute or entertaining. By the time they reached the silver balls, she'd had enough. Her wine was definitely gone, and now she was just in the room, thinking about the sex. Thinking about the excessively good sex. And not the tree. And not the kids. But definitely about how meaning-less it was. She was. All this was. He probably didn't care, he'd never wanted to do all this any-way, so he was just good at acting. As he'd been good at acting last night.

Breaking. Point.

She hung a silver ball on the closest empty bough and, when she went toward the boxes of ornaments, just kept going. Past. Toward the stairs.

She'd reached the first step down when he caught her. "Where are you going?"

"Tell them I went to the outhouse and the hogs ate me."

"Huh?"

Okay, maybe the wine hadn't completely worn off. Or maybe it just gave the illusion of control to be the one to start making fun of herself be-fore someone else got the chance.

"You have to tell me what is wrong." He gave her a little shake. "We've been over the Lyons thing. We've been over how awful I am at help-ing people. If you don't tell me, I'll be no use. And I want to be of use. I don't like you looking like I just murdered your best friend."

"Don't do that." She tried to jerk free again, but he had strong hands, and wasn't letting go. "You don't get to holler that I'm entirely meaningless to you and then act like you give a damn."

"I never said that."

"Yes, you did." The pointy shape of the toes of her boots seeped into her consciousness, and for a brief second she considered kicking him in the shins with those pointy toes. He'd probably let her go then.

"I did not." He dragged her back from the stairs and released her in the direction of the wall so she'd have to go past him to get to the stairs or the elevator.

"Lyons was going on about how I was a conniver who was after your money, and you said back that I didn't matter at all."

"I meant to the conversation we were having." He shoved his hands through his hair. "We need to go back there and finish the tree."

"You finish it."

"I'm not going to finish it alone."

"Just going to go back and tell the kids I'm being irrational? I know, you could tell them I'm drunk. I drank wine before I came over, enough to give me a tiny bit of extra strength that I need to get through an evening with you, pretending like everything is okay. Well, guess what, it's not okay. I'm not okay. And this was a huge mistake."

To his credit, he held his hands up in a way meant to calm her, to unwind the situation somehow, but it was too late for that.

"It was only going to be temporary anyway." She gestured with one hand. "Let me through. I've gotta go hail a cab."

When he rubbed his head, he looked almost distraught enough for her to buy this act. "I'll take you home if that's what you want, but we're not done."

He didn't offer to go end the video, just left it running as he gestured for her to walk down the stairs, as she'd been intending, and fell into step beside her.

He was just there, grabbing her coat, grabbing his, and all she could think was that he'd ruined her day, the least he could do was drive her home. But then she remembered she'd have to be in a car with him for a good twenty minutes to get there.

"I'll just get a cab."

"No, you'll shut it and let me drive you home. If you don't, I'll follow you home and bang on your door until the neighbors call the cops."

"You won't. You hate scandal."

"I don't give a damn what your neighbors think of me."

"You mean you don't care if it's someone else suffering the stares and whispers." She pulled her coat on, buttoned up and stuffed her hands into much less fancy gloves than the ones he'd dragged out. "But whatever, drive me home. Say whatever it is you want to say in the car, because you're not coming in."

CHAPTER TWELVE

A COUPLE OF minutes later, Wolfe opened the passenger door of his car for Angel to get in, silently working on how to turn this happy parade around.

Once they'd both settled, he started the engine, asked her address and got on with it.

She'd demanded he tell her what was on his mind in the car, but he needed more time. Right now, the only thing he had room for was a desire to fix this so strong it blotted out everything else.

She sat in silence, staring out of the window, as she might in a taxi. Cold rolled off her. The set of her jaw and her silence suggested anger, but the way she hugged herself with her arms said hurt. He'd *hurt* her. Inadvertently, but there it was. Something he'd never learned how to fix.

They made the drive without speaking. By the time they'd arrived, all he had in the form of a plan was to apologize. Maybe pour out her wine.

He parked in front of her building and got out to open her door, but she'd already sprung out and was hurrying to the building.

Her slick, winter-unfriendly boots worked in his favor. He caught her arm as she slid and although she gave him a *look* for his trouble, she didn't try to get free. Until they were inside. Then she disengaged her arm and resumed speed walking.

Inside the building, the differences between what he saw and what he'd expected to see jarred.

No doorman. It wasn't a bad part of town, but she didn't enjoy the kind of lifestyle of her peers.

The elevator seemed rickety. It moved slowly and groaned as it passed each floor. Something else that failed to inspire confidence.

Once off, she hurried again, with him on her heels.

"Still determined to come inside?"

"I told you we were going to talk," he said. Not as if he could screw up talking to her any worse than talking to Lyons, not when this had already spiraled to the point of damage control.

The lights inside were low, just bright enough to see the utter lack of decor in her little apartment.

The silence extended. She turned on lights and

took off her coat. Going through the motions, then walked into the little kitchen he could see from the hallway.

She'd been so angry at his house, but now, she just seemed sad. And withdrawn. Almost as if she'd managed to ignore him being there altogether.

And none of what he saw made him feel any better.

He followed her into the kitchen for his own glass of wine, past the main focus of her furnishings: bookcases lined with books.

A sofa. A desk. And the one oddity that made him feel a little better: a gorgeous sapphire gown wrapped in plastic, hanging from the top corner of the most accessible bookcase.

She eyed him—specifically noting that he'd removed his coat—and returned with her wine to the tiny living room. "Just say whatever you wanna say."

"I want to say I'm sorry," he said without preamble, because he had no preamble. He had no bloody idea what he was supposed to say.

"Okay." She wasn't buying it.

"Your dress is beautiful," he tried again. "I'll be happy to see you in it."

Her expression softened a little, but she still looked…lost.

"I didn't know what to get. I just went to the shop, told them where I was goin' and bought what they said. Some of what they said," she amended. "They had a lot in mind. Jewelry. A real pretty, beaded clutch that looked like peacock feathers, but it was crazy expensive."

She still worried about money.

As much as he wanted to know about her, and he did, seeing inside her worries sucked.

She didn't sit, but she did drink her glass of wine down, as if she needed it to be in his presence. Sex only made things awkward when there were expectations shattered, had been his experience. They'd had no expectations for one another last night, except that they'd enjoy the time together. Which he had, until it had gone wrong, and he suspected that was why she was reacting so poorly now to Lyons's unfortunately pointed outburst earlier.

"Look, I don't know what the hell is going on. I get that it hurt to hear me and Lyons fighting about you, but it wasn't really about you. He doesn't trust anyone anymore. He really doesn't trust women. And I told you I'm terrible at relationships, at knowing what to say. Ever."

"You said that."

"Tell me what you want me to say. You know I'm no' a bad guy, you know I'm rubbish at talking about things. Throw me a line here…"

"You hate scandal. You told me you hate drama at work. You don't let things contaminate the work environment." She drained her wine glass, set it carefully on a shelf on the closest bookcase.

"Right."

"Right," she repeated. "Then explain to me how you could have this discussion at work about me, where anyone could hear. Where I heard and stayed put to listen to, kind of so I could head off anyone else who come down the hall. People I work with every day and who already don't care too much for me. Tell me that."

"Tell you how I got dragged into an argument?"

"Why did you go talk to him? Why didn't you leave once he made clear that was how the conversation was gonna go? Didn't it bother you at all?"

He drank down his own wine and sat on her sofa; standing up seemed like entirely too much effort when it took all his concentration to be in the conversation.

"It bothered me, but once it began to go that direction—which was pretty much from the moment he walked in—I didn't know how to stop it. Just like I don't know how to stop *this*."

"I'm not being irrational."

"No. You're not, but you are angry and hurt. I didn't mean that to happen. And I don't know how to fix it."

"Explain it."

He rubbed a hand over his face and leaned back. "I went to talk to him about you. I wanted to see what he was thinking when he said those things to you. But we never got to that."

"Why?"

"Because he greeted me, kind of, and then launched into an attack about the shenanigans."

"Why?"

"I don't know." Wolfe heard his voice rising and took a breath. "Before the shooting—hell, before he started griping at me today, I would've said he hated the spectacle as much as I do. But then he created a spectacle, which shows how well I know him."

"He said I was using you."

"If I knew what that was about, I'd tell you. I've had thirty-four years to get to know him and the only explanation I have is the history we both have with our parents." How did the conversation get around to this? "Did you look them up?"

She shook her head.

"Not interested?"

"Felt too much like gossip. People don't go to tabloids for accuracy." She spoke a little less carefully. The massive glass of wine had kicked in. She slouched on the arm of the sofa. "And it shouldn't matter, what your people are like. Should only matter what you're like."

"I agree." But he was starting to see that it mattered in a way. It mattered when trying to understand Lyons's behavior, and his. And hers.

"You're lookin' mighty hard at the bookcases."

"I'm trying to figure out if you've started packing already."

She looked over the apartment, which—aside from the brilliant deep blue gown—was quite flat in color. Nothing like her, with her blues and pinks. It didn't match.

She took a moment to answer. She took such a moment that she actually walked away from him, to sit on the sofa properly where she could unzip the boots she'd worn and ease them off. Below, she had on outrageously colorful socks, which had never been seen with the lovely, delicate white dress with frosty blue flowers.

Colorful. Unlike her apartment.

"I haven't started packing. This is it." She tucked her boots around the corner of the sofa, out of the way. "He was right about somethin'. I'm not like you. I know you're used to church mansions and sleeping beneath the glow of stained-glass windows. But for me, this is..."

She paused, head tilting as if she was considering whether to continue that statement, or maybe even trying to figure out what the end was.

He couldn't tell. But he still prompted. "It's what?"

"It's very nice by my system of measurement," she said softly, shrugging. "The roof doesn't leak. The heat is pretty great. I don't have to put wood in the fire every four hours to keep the pipes from bursting, or never sleep a full night through the winter because I must wake and tend the fire. I don't have to watch the woodpile shrink and wonder if it will be enough to hold out until more money comes in to buy more."

She'd had a wood budget? His entire life, he'd never considered anything remotely like that. It made the apartment quite different seeing it through her eyes and explained why she'd been so terrified of his home at first. And it became painfully clear that this was a landmine he wasn't prepared for.

"Lyons knows I grew up poor. That's why he said I'm after your money."

"Lyons says that kind of thing about a lot of people. You could've been middle-class for generations, and he'd still think that," he muttered. "It wasn't always like that, but since the shooting, he just seems to jump to the worst possible conclusion about everyone. Patients. Coworkers. Even me. Then rants about having to protect me."

"What was that about?"

He could only shrug. "I don't remember him protecting me in the last decade. What I remember is him resenting me trying to protect him after the shooting. That's it."

"He needs to talk to someone."

"I keep saying that." Wolfe looked down the sofa, then stood and moved closer to her. "Are you leaving New York to save money?"

"No."

"Then why?"

"Haven't you ever felt like you didn't belong somewhere?" She looked so stricken he wanted to say yes. But places weren't his problem. His problem was belonging with someone specific. Anyone, actually. Even his brother, he'd been recently reminded.

This line of questioning was foolish. The only thing he could say to comfort her would be the kind of thing he'd say to convince her to stay, and he couldn't do that. "I came here to get out from under the weight of my family's reputation, so in a way, I did. Here, no one knows them. I'm just some Scot who talks funny."

"And who lives in a fancy church house."

She was still intimidated by that.

"You could start small…get a vase you don't mind breaking." He gestured to the table. "Or anything you like to make it homier. I know you can afford a little more luxury than you're allowing yourself."

"I don't like to spend money like that," she admitted, then shrugged. "I don't really have it to spend either."

"Why? Student loans?"

"That," she agreed, "and I send money to my grandmother. I don't speak to my family, but she's elderly and needs the money. So, I send it."

And kept her lifestyle small here to provide for people she didn't speak to anymore. Whatever Lyons thought he knew about her, he was wrong. She was good. Anyone could see it. Even a fool like him.

Asking why she didn't speak to them seemed too much for this unsteady conversation.

"I missed you after you left last night. And looked forward to seeing you tonight." He casually took her hand where it had been sitting on the sofa between them and before he could think it through added, "Going to miss you when you're gone, I think."

Her eyes went wide, but then she smiled, just a touch, just a little hope-filled lifting of the corners of her mouth.

Then he realized how the statement sounded, and added, "You have to admit that the sex was astonishingly good."

The frank statement made her cheeks flash instantly red, and she shrugged, losing the smile and not saying anything in response, but it clearly shifted her attention from the unfortunate admission.

"If you don't agree, I'm going to go into vivid, mouth-watering detail."

A short sound, almost as if a laugh and a breath got confused, puffed from her, and she blushed. Really blushed. "Fine, it was good."

"Imagine how much incredibly hot sex we could have if I wasn't half-robot, half-jester and you weren't a bucket of insecurities."

Her frown was instantaneous. "I'm not a bucket of insecurities."

She didn't pull her hand away, so he kept going.

With a look. A very pointed, skeptical look that she mirrored for all of three seconds before rolling her eyes toward the ceiling.

"Okay, I'm a little bucket. Like a beach pail."

"For the sake of class, I'll say you're a wine barrel of insecurities, and I'm what happens when you cross a court jester with a calculator."

She finally laughed for him.

Unwilling to miss his opportunity, he cupped a hand around her jaw and tugged her to meet him as he leaned in, and kissed her. Not the kind of kiss he wanted—the kind where the whole world went blurry and physics stopped being a thing that mattered—but something sweet. Affectionate. And needed.

That warmth was there, but it was something more. Almost like relief. As if he'd been tense since last night when she'd left so abruptly, and the stiffness that had lingered in his whole body dissolved into her sofa.

Pulling back enough to see her, he had to ask, because he wasn't sure. He wasn't sure about anything when it came to her. "Are we good?"

She paused only for a second, then nodded.

"Not angry with me anymore?"

No pause then, just a shake of her head.

"Good, because I didn't like it." He followed up his statement with a much gentler, sweeter kiss. "And I really didn't like that you were hurt."

"Me either," she whispered. "I'm usually so careful."

So careful she kept everyone away. There was much more here to figure out about Angel, and for the first time, he really wanted to know. This shortened time frame wasn't without any risks, he knew now he could screw it up, but he wanted to take advantage of it while she was there. To try.

"I didn't sleep much, and the wine tonight... Would you be offended if I kicked you out now?"

"Don't want me to stay?" He wanted her to say yes. He wanted her to lock the door, show him her little bedroom and lie there with him until morning.

"I don't think it's a good idea."

Either she didn't want to hurt his feelings, or

she really did want him to stay and also thought it was a bad idea. Maybe both.

"All right." He had made great headway tonight. Soon, she'd tell him the rest. She'd tell him whatever had ostracized her from her family, while compelling her to support them still. She'd tell him why she hid so hard from people, because she'd accomplished so much in her life already, people would judge her on that, not some silly accent or stereotype, and he'd figure out how to help.

"You know, we still have time for loads of amazing sex before you leave New York." He swung his coat on and fished out the keys but grinned at her.

"What about your brother?"

"I'm *not* inviting him to the amazing sex parties," he announced, probably too loudly in the little apartment. "He's so boring, and I'm greedy. I don't share."

She just shook her head and gave him a good-natured shove toward the door.

"Okay, then. Goodnight."

He snagged her by the waist for another kiss before she shoved him out and gave her a brief lecture about engaging all the locks and making certain her windows were locked up too. Then stayed outside her door until he heard four distinct clicks and the chain slide into place.

The next evening, Angel eased into the front seat of Wolfe's fancy car and arranged her gown for least wrinkling, making all efforts to be as presentable as possible for her first ball. Which had included an earlier trip to the salon for hair-styling and professionally applied make-up.

Professional make-up had been necessary after she'd lain awake half the night, trying to figure out what to do, what she could stand doing. What she could risk for him. Make-up gave an extra bit of courage in the form of under-eye concealer.

She glanced his way, watching him steer and shift. Watching his legs move beneath the kilt. Because he'd gone and done it, worn a kilt with a black tie and jacket. Probably to torture her and every other human who got a sexy thrill from a good tartan above manly, muscled legs.

"You're quiet," he said, giving her an excuse to look at him, and the legs, which made her once again regret having asked him to go last night.

"I'm nervous," she admitted, but didn't explain that the ball wasn't even the biggest chunk of her nerves right now. She'd terrified herself with her intent.

"Afraid you're going to lose control and attack me on the dance floor?" he teased, then looked at her and sobered. "There'll be no breakables worth worrying about. Really."

The breakables weren't the only thing to be nervous about tonight. After their fight, he'd gone out of his way to try and make things right between them. Twice, actually, and there was just no way around that for her. He'd made her feel important to him. And every time she'd shown him a glimpse of what she kept hidden, he still hadn't turned her away. He truly seemed to want to know, and not in a way that made her heart jackrabbit against her ribs.

But his manly muscled legs did enough of that.

He'd said he'd miss her and had clearly not meant to say it, the best kind of confession. Spontaneous truth was better than any specially crafted sentiment. It made her want to be real with him. She'd labored over the decision half the night because she'd finally accepted she loved him, and if she went to Atlanta, it wasn't New York or her job that she'd miss. She'd mourn the loss of *him*. But the only way she could stay would be to risk him knowing and rejecting. Tell him the truth.

All of it.

His reaction would make the decision for her, whether she should go or if she could try to stay.

He pulled up in front of the towering hotel where Sutcliffe's annual winter charity ball was hosted, but, before he got out, reached behind his seat to retrieve a lovely box wrapped in blue paper and silver ribbon, smile on his face.

"While we wait for the valet, I got you something."

Her belly did an excited little flip. He'd bought her a gift? "What is it?"

"The only Christmas gift I'm giving this year," he said, and two thoughts popped into her head.

Don't read too much into it.

And, *I didn't get him a gift.*

"Why?"

"Because I wanted to." He waited for her to open it.

The idea of packages—man, she loved getting packages. Online shopping was pretty much the only reason she got packages these days, but they still thrilled her. So much, she felt the need to dawdle, to drag out tearing into the paper, even if that was a foot into the conversation she'd planned.

Those nervous belly critters sprang to life again and she continued the delay, just so she had a second to breathe first. "It's not Christmas yet."

"I know." He watched her with steadiness, but fidgeted with the button on the gear shift, giving himself away. He was nervous too. Trying not to make it too big a deal, but unable to completely hide how excited he was to have her open it.

It was that flash of little-boy excitement that evaporated her own fears. She pulled the silver ribbon and lifted the lid.

Inside, nestled in matching silver tissue paper, sat the beaded peacock handbag. The grotesquely expensive handbag that made her heart thud like a little materialistic consumer.

"Wolfe…"

"That's the one, right?"

She nodded her answer, mouth too busy for that one word. "How did you find it? I didn't tell you what shop it was at."

Gingerly, she lifted it free and opened the delicate silver clasp to peer into the deep sapphire lining within. Probably handmade. And that lining looked like silk… The most beautiful thing she'd ever seen up close, and it was hers.

"It wasn't that hard. Don't be too impressed." He took her chin and leaned over to give her the smallest kiss. "It matches your dress. Shop lady knew what she was about."

Her throat thickened, and she was momentarily glad for the confines of the car. The burning in her eyes said she'd probably have thrown herself into his arms and cried like an idiot if she'd been able to move.

"Thank you." The words were pale in comparison to what she actually felt, stand-in words for emotion she didn't have a name for. This wasn't a pity gift. Not a box of canned vegetables left on her stoop by the ladies' group at the local church. Not something she'd picked up for herself. And it was better because of him, because he'd cared enough to go out and find it for her, no matter what he said.

The valet approached, leaving her precious little time to transfer her cell and keys from the little pouch she'd stashed in his car into the bag.

The door opened, and she climbed out to find Wolfe there, spectacular in his kilt, and had to shake her head again. "Blue and red tartan—we kind of match."

His brows popped up and the grin he gave her set her innards jiggling, but then his elbow came out to escort.

The building was an art deco masterpiece, as New York as was possible to be in her mind. Fluid geometry and graceful designs in black, gold and a deep, warm ochre that tracked patterns across the lobby, past the tree-shaped conical poinsettia displays.

There would definitely be things she could break here, and never be able to pay back.

"Don't panic," he murmured, quietly enough that only she would hear as he led them in the direction the signs pointed, laying his free hand over the one she clutched at his elbow with.

"I'm all right," she answered, then smiled up at him so he'd see the truth. "I am. I'm not sure why, but it was just a fleeting thought."

But one he'd somehow heard, or just knew enough about her now to suspect. Knew enough and still came with her. Still gave her a beautiful present. Everything would be all right.

They'd gotten there early enough for the short video they broadcast for the kids, and a few awkward snapshots she wanted to believe wouldn't look completely hokey and sent to her feed without dwelling on how adoringly she looked at him in every image.

Inside the ballroom, it was all twinkling lights, champagne towers and music. Checkerboard tiles on the perimeter of the floor gave way to an intricate floral design in the center, where people danced. No, where they *waltzed*. This was the kind of gathering where you were expected to know a particular dance, not just hold on and sway.

"You're quiet," he said, leading her to a table and urging her down there.

"I'm a little overwhelmed."

"No reason for that." He sounded so confident. Not at all worried, but then he didn't know the words she was about to drag out of her guts.

She opened her mouth to say something, but her voice caught. Rasped. Sounded pained. She coughed. "I thought we could talk about something."

He held up one finger. "Hold that thought. I'll get drinks."

"I want to tell you something," she said to the air, watching his back and his broad shoulders as he made his way to the bar, then said the words to herself, under her breath. Practice, even though she'd practiced in her mind all day, unable to say them out loud.

"I want to tell you about my family."

Want wasn't the right word. She really didn't *want* to tell him these things. She'd like to continue never speaking about it all. *Need* was the word she was looking for.

No one else paid her any mind; she tried again, repeating a whispered confession in a room of dazzling twinkle lights and music that rose goosebumps over her flesh.

"I have a criminal record," she whispered to herself again.

Then, "I went to jail."

He would accept her. He had to accept her. This strange, powerful lifting in her chest was the reason people took chances with their hearts.

It might also be the reason people threw up on their dates...

A deep, fortifying breath, and she let herself watch the manly swagger of his return, wine glass in each hand, sucked in by the twinkle in his eyes as he handed the glass to her. "I will cut you off if you start shouting."

"I'm not angry." No, she was terrified. If she got loud right now, it'd more likely be one of those horror-movie screams that made the dog's ears bleed.

She took a sip of the rosé, traced her fingertips over the swirls of beading on the peacock bag he'd given her, summoning her courage.

The clutch meant he cared. There was no reason to search it out except to make her happy. Maybe he even felt this Christmas could be different, something special for them both, and make up for a lifetime of disappointment and heartbreak.

Worry must've been painted on her face, because he leaned in and kissed her cheek while placing his large, strong hand over hers tracing the beadwork. "You had something on your mind, remember?"

Gentle voice. Tender touch. Sweet eyes.

She leaned to place the pretty, mostly full glass in the center of the table, where she couldn't accidentally break it, then turned her hand over and clasped his. The quivering of her belly turning into a small earthquake tremor, but she said anyway, "I need to tell you something."

Either he felt her shaking, or she looked too serious. The playful light in his eyes dimmed, and after he looked at their joined hands, met her gaze again. No words passed his lips, he didn't nod his head or give any indication whether he wanted her to continue, he just held her gaze—his brow firming in a way that made clear he was listening.

"About my family."

CHAPTER THIRTEEN

THE MOMENT ANGEL announced a need to confess whatever her family secret was, Wolfe got a strange kind of tunnel vision. He could hear the music, tasteful and loud enough to make their conversation private, but the emotion suddenly twisting his guts into knots was impossible to mistake for anything but fear.

Which made no sense. He *wanted* to know about her because he wanted to help, but the gravity of whatever she was about to share with him that hurt her every day came into sharp focus. Knowing was a responsibility. She needed him to say the right things to whatever she shared. God help him, he wanted that too, but already knew he was going to mess it up. He always messed it up.

The wine in his stomach soured. If he didn't get up and move around, he might get sick.

"Let's go find somewhere else to talk." A foolish request, a way to claim a little more time to think, to prepare himself. "Don't you want to go somewhere private? We could just leave. I mean, we've done our appearance. Let's say good evening to Alberts, then just get out of here."

"You don't want to dance? I thought that was why you wanted a date." The bewildered look in her eyes and the fear blooming behind it stilled his flight. She wanted to be there in a way, she'd gotten dressed up and truly was just the loveliest woman under normal circumstances, but in that dress, with her silky, dark hair swept to the side and that sapphire lace, a neckline that seemed built to draw attention to her pale, freckled shoulders and delicate collarbone… She was exquisite. She should get to enjoy it.

"Dance, then," he agreed, because it gave him another moment. He rose and offered a hand, immediately sweeping her onto the dance floor. At least there he could get an arm around her waist and hold her closer than was generally socially acceptable, and that helped his sudden nerves.

With the new bag in one hand, and his hand in the other, she tucked in close, her head tilted back to look up at him, determination in the tilt of her chin.

"You sure you want to do this here?" He had

to ask again, because the light in her eyes, which he loved seeing filled with warmth or sparkling with amusement, now looked determined, but afraid. He could see her own fear that he'd mess it up lurking in the bent of her brows.

"It's okay," she answered, the cool surface of the beaded peacock feather of her bag, pressed against the nape of his neck, chilling him. He pulled her closer and schooled his features to something level and—he hoped—supportive.

"I said I don't speak with them, but it's more like they don't speak with me." She blew out a slow breath. "I don't really disagree with their decision, but it was their decision."

The people she sent money didn't speak with her? "Why do you support them?"

"Because my father has been in jail even longer than he would've been because of me." She swallowed, and the little hand tucked into his tightened. She was afraid he was going to just run away as soon as she told him?

Her father was in jail, and she got his sentence lengthened?

"Why is he in jail?"

"Felony larceny."

Theft, his mind swapped out the legal jargon

for the common crime name. "He pinched something and you reported him?"

"Sort of."

She looked away then, and he knew this wasn't coming any easier to her than it came to him to listen to it.

"I went to jail for him first." With her head turned away, it took him a few seconds to realize what she said, and then his guts seized up, as if there were no movement in his body at all.

"I don't understand." And he wasn't sure he wanted to understand. How could she be a doctor if she'd been convicted of a felony?

"My dad never bought presents. He never bought anything if he could steal it." She lightly explained, glossing over details, filtering. Either still protecting herself or considering the damage her confession could do and still forcing each word. "If he had a present for me for my birthday or Christmas, he'd stolen it. I figured out when I was about twelve, and I stopped accepting his gifts."

The music shifted to something slower yet, and he guided her other hand to his neck. It had started to tremble and if he didn't need to hold it, he could put both his arms around her. Not the best dancing, but something simple he could do. He could mostly control his body, even when words failed him.

"When I was fifteen, he broke into a nice house in the area while the family was away and took a laptop. It was wonderful, and I wanted it so badly… I *pretended* he hadn't stolen it, that he'd just bought it for me because he loved me—even though he'd probably used money from other things he'd stolen and sold, but he'd *bought* it. Only he hadn't."

And she turned him in, Wolfe finished in his head. Why was she taking so long to say it? *Just say it.*

"I was in the library when the true owner saw me with it and the custom floral case and called the sheriff."

"They arrested you?"

"They took me to the sheriff's office, confiscated the laptop, then grilled me about where I'd gotten it. My dad had been in jail recently for something else, and I knew if I told the truth, if I said my father had given it to me, he'd go back for a long time. That put everything at risk for the whole family, me included. Food. Water. Power…"

Firewood. That story came back at him, every word conjuring images he didn't want to see. A young Angel, scared, probably too thin. Ragged clothes. In a place that was always cold and in need of firewood. The woman who'd tried to wash off her freckles because she'd thought them dirt.

He didn't want to know this.

For some reason, he still asked, "What did you do?"

"I told them I had stolen it. I knew where the girl lived. It wasn't hard to concoct a story."

He saw the horror in his eyes reflected by the flash of fear in her eyes. "Do you want me to stop?" she asked, and then began pulling away.

"Wait." He tightened his arms, at first to bring her back into his embrace fully, but then tighter, to feel her soft, warm body pressed against him. She was actually safe now. As long as no one found out and put her license in jeopardy. Why didn't the authorities already know? They did background checks before licensing.

The rest of the room receded a little when she pressed against him again, and he could look into her eyes. "Tell me, quickly. Like ripping off a bandage. Tell me fast."

She was still afraid, her chest rose and fell too quickly, but she nodded, eyes too wide. "I confessed so my family would be better taken care

of, but while I was in the juvenile detention fa-
cility, my will began to crumble. They began
visiting me, reminding me that as a first-time
offender, and an honor student, I would get leni-
ency, but he'd get a long sentence. All of them,
my two uncles, my aunt, my cousin. Eventually
they even brought down Meemaw."

She'd stopped swaying. Or maybe he'd stopped
them. They stood still to one side of the dance
floor, and he knew that worry on his face gave
him away.

"So, I did it. I pled guilty and went to juvie
for two months."

"Before you turned him in to get out?"

"No. I did the whole sentence, took the probation." She breathed slowly, her words still sounding forced. "But he ended up in jail before that
was done for something else and was going to be
gone a long time. It was a long time to think, and
I came to see that having this lie on my record
would keep me from achieving my own goals.
Part of my probation involved a social worker
and she was very kind, so I told her. She took
an interest in me."

In Angelica.

"She told the court and it was taken care of?"

"I had to provide my journals from the time,

showing I'd actually been away when the theft occurred. Then they looked closer and found details that led to his conviction."

"And this increased his prison time."

She nodded, and then took a deep breath. "And he's still in. And life is still hard for them."

So, she sent them money.

There was more to it, he could tell there was more to it, but this was enough. He didn't know what to do with it. Or why it meant she was moving.

"I'm sorry that happened to you," he said. What else was he supposed to say? He couldn't fix that. This was what she'd told her ex? This had gotten her fired? "Does Alberts know?"

"My record was expunged," she said softly, shaking her head.

Thank God for that. "So…do you feel better?"

She swallowed, then licked her lips, holding his gaze with a kind of desperate kneading of the back of his neck. "It's not just him. It's the whole family. We have a reputation. You moved away from your parents' reputation, I did too. I know that when I don't concentrate on keeping my language proper and clean, I slip into the colloquialisms and lazy diction of my native tongue, and it marks me as *other* to most people. It's a slippery slope. Once you know where to look, a lot can be found out. And people are nosy, especially if they think you don't belong. They'd look. People also wouldn't understand me continuing to send money, which is kind of enabling their criminal existence, but I do it, and I'm not going to stop."

"Because you feel guilty."

"Because I feel *responsible*. And I know what it is to go without. I've left out a lot—it could take a lifetime of therapy to go over—I just want you to know that, even though I'm broken, and I don't trust easily, I trust *you*. And…"

Ice shot through his chest. No. This wasn't supposed to be about him. He let go and stepped back, hands up to try and stop this, or slow it down. Because of the pregnant pause at the end of her statement. She trusted him, and…

"Angel, we should go," he said. They hadn't been dancing really anyway, just sort of swaying and having conversations far too intense for a dance floor. Especially when he saw plainly written on her face what the next declaration was going to be.

"I can't stop now," she said, following his retreat, until she grabbed his hands and that stopped him. "I just need to get it out."

"Darlin', it's not… I don't…"

"I don't want to leave. I want to stay here and be with you. Have all the fantastic sex." She tried to laugh, but it was the whiffle of breath that rattled in her chest and up her throat. Trying to be playful when terrified. "I love you. I just need to know if you can accept that this is where I come from, that these are the things that made me…that I'm one of *those* Conleys of Tarpin… Terrapin Hollow."

Tarpin Holler. The words he'd thought she'd said early on, and then covered with something that sounded more sensible somehow.

"Angel." He pulled one hand free, rubbed his face, then the back of his neck to keep it from snapping, so brittle and tense with the need to run. "I wouldn't have gotten involved if you weren't leaving. If you're staying, I can't."

"Can't what? Accept this? Accept me?"

"I told you, I don't know how to have a relationship. All this makes anything I say to you able to hurt you badly, and I have done that in the past. I don't want to do it with you. You want to go to Atlanta, you've said so many times."

"I thought I couldn't be happy if I stayed here, but if you can accept me, that's all I need."

Acceptance. Acceptance. It wasn't about that.

But she was a doctor too, she had the same instinct to heal that he had. She'd try to fix *him*,
and be hurt more in the process. He had a duty
to do no harm. Or at least only harm in a surgical manner meant to stave off more damage.

"I don't want you to stay." The only way he
could think to soften it was to leave out talk of
acceptance and past wounds, to just bring it to
the bottom line. "If you stay, I have to go."

He didn't need to look her in the eyes to know
they were wet and couldn't bring himself to
look. "I'll drive you home."

Where she could pack and save herself again.

Atlanta would be better for her.

A rustle of skirts was his answer, and he lifted
his eyes to an empty spot before him, and her
hurrying toward the door.

He stepped back and felt something crunch
under his heel.

"Get up!" Lyons's barking voice broke through
Wolfe's sleepy haze, and the sensation of someone whacking his leg with something.

"Get tae!" he growled back, in his still-half-
drunken state and not wanting to deal with his
brother gloating. Or telling him what he was

doing wrong. Or telling him again to grow up. Or telling him anything.

"Get up," Lyons repeated, and Wolfe heard him drag a chair over toward the bed. A peek confirmed his brother settling in. "It's past noon."

He didn't care if it was past noon. Or if he'd lost a whole week. Sleeping was a comfort right now; whiskey had just facilitated the comfort of oblivion.

"What do you want? Say it and get out."

Another thing he didn't care about right now? If he pushed Lyons's conflict buttons and this all went as badly as he'd feared with every interaction since the shooting.

"You sent me a text then didn't answer any of the three I sent you. So, get up."

Wolfe had heard his phone pinging earlier, he just hadn't cared about that either.

A full look at Lyons confirmed him sitting with that judgmental stare.

If this was going to happen, it would happen with him upright, not flat on his back from the invisible truck that had driven him over.

When he pulled himself up, he grumbled, "What do you want?"

"I want to know what happened with Conley."

"I told you to leave her be." Wolfe stood up, crossed to his bureau and dug out a pair of pajama bottoms to make himself partially decent.

"I wasn't planning on going after her."

"You weren't planning on it, but you still act like a complete ass all the time. I'm tired of walking eggshells round you," Wolfe almost shouted, then all the alcohol-diluted blood in his body rushed into his head in one massive throb. His hand flew to cover one temple, as if that would keep his head from exploding, and he lowered his voice. "I know last Christmas was the worst of a long line of bad Christmases. I know it's changed who you are, and I've been trying to figure out how to help you get back to yourself. But I'm done. With all of it."

"Good," Lyons said.

"You need to get *your* mind right. I say that with love, and *frustration*, because we're not okay. We probably *both* need therapy, if we're being honest here." He stopped, all will to speak leaving and taking with it the tension that always snaked over him when he got involved in important, personal conversations. Talking with her had been like that. At least at first.

"I hired an investigator after we spoke."

Wolfe cut him off, not wanting to hear him slag Angel. "I know she was in juvenile detention."

"And you're still reeking over her?"

"I love her," Wolfe barked again, giving his head another tooth-shattering pulse with the words he hadn't even been able to admit to himself.

In contrast, Lyons took a breath and spoke patiently, even gently, "She's a criminal. Her license will be gone when the board finds out."

Lyons had patience suddenly? Well, Wolfe had none left. If he was threatening her...

"Shut it. You're not telling anyone. She took the blame for her father's crime to try and protect her family. I know you tried to protect me when you could growing up, I know you're trying now, in your way, but you leave her be."

"The lot of them are criminals, Wolfe. The whole lot."

"She's not. She's a good person, and she's leaving..." His voice actually broke when he said that, and he had to take a minute to try and shove that horrible ache from his chest before he could think of another thing. It was worse than when his head tried to split in half. "I know I can't have her. I know she's better off with someone else."

Lyons wasn't losing control of himself, Wolfe thought again, despite him basically telling him he was broken and all the things he'd been dancing around for a year out of fear of making matters worse.

No, that wasn't right. That wasn't what he was feeling. That wasn't what had held him back.

It wasn't fear of making things worse—though he'd had some of that too—he hadn't said important things out of fear of *alienating* his only brother. Of losing what tiny bit there was of family and connection.

"You're not angry?" he asked finally, jumping subject as he swiveled back to where Lyons still sat, elbows on his knees, in a fairly relaxed posture.

"I'm not best pleased, but no. No' really. I know you're upset," Lyons said quietly. "Tell me you don't really love her, you poor bastard."

"Wish I could." Wolfe finally sat back down on the corner of his bed. "You came here to try and sort me out."

"I came here to check on you," Lyons corrected, shaking his head. "I know we're not so close as family should be, but I do worry about you. I care what happens to you. And I will, no matter how many stupid mistakes you make, trusting—or loving—people you shouldn't."

"Then why's it got to be so hard to talk? It's always hard to talk." Except to Angel.

"Because we're broken, and there's no fixing it. We are what they made us, and some other rotten misfortune." Lyons half repeated his words back, but what he added... It was wrong. Nearly what he'd said to Angel, but not so hope-filled as when she'd turned it back to him. *These are the broken pieces that made me, can you accept them?* Because she'd already accepted that he was bad at relationships.

She'd accepted his flaws enough to risk herself. And he'd rejected her for his own flaws. Had he said that?

No.

He loved his brother, but he didn't want to become him. Even though, when Wolfe looked at him again, he saw the smallest quirk of a grin. Rueful. But present. First time in a long time. Enough to give him hope.

Lyons wasn't going anywhere after all that.

He wasn't losing his mind in a fit of rage.

He didn't even look angry.

Then he said words Wolfe would've never thought to hear. "You've got it back to front, little brother. She's not the one who's better off, but maybe the damage is already done. You're going to suffer for her now or suffer for her later."

Early Sunday morning, well before the hours of decency, Angel called Alberts's emergency contact phone number. She hadn't been asleep from the night before, and she couldn't sleep until she got some things sorted out. Her mind just wouldn't stop spinning in circles, and every one came back around to the horror she'd seen on Wolfe's handsome face.

He'd tried to spin it as something else, the old *It's not you, it's me* nonsense. But she knew better.

All she'd actually done after having fled the ball like a pathetic version of Cinderella—she'd even lost her bag with phone and keys, probably in the taxi—was get her super to open the door, report her cell lost, change out of her dress and sit. She did the things she had to do and spent the rest of the night figuring out what she was *supposed* to do now. Run? Hide? If she was going to survive December, she couldn't be bumping into him in the halls, or Jenna's room. She didn't want to see Lyons either.

The peacock bag didn't suit her anyway. It

was made for the kind of woman who attended those events. She was more suited to something made of pleather and available at big box stores.

Sunday night, after sleeping during the day with the help of her partially empty wines, she clocked in for her first night shift. For her remaining weeks at Sutcliffe, she'd be on nights— a really crappy schedule to volunteer for, but one that might save what was left of her dignity. If the night rotation had even watched their live streams, they would've seen a stranger they didn't already know as timid and standoffish. They most likely wouldn't have had any opinion of her at all.

It would be better on nights. Even losing her Sunday in order to get started was okay. One less night to mourn, a way to keep busy. It was easier to keep her mask in place when no one was there, poking at it with their eyes full of judgment or pity while she tried to keep her chin up.

January sat on the horizon. She could make it. She'd survived worse.

When you fell down you had to get up. In real life, no one came to carry you from the ice.

That had been a Christmas fairy tale.

CHAPTER FOURTEEN

AFTER THE THREE days it took to finally adjust to a nightshift schedule, not much could drag Angel into Sutcliffe during the day, but a message from Jenna announcing her discharge did it.

She'd bought *her* only Christmas present after work yesterday morning and hadn't had a chance to deliver it. When she'd gotten home this morning, before she'd even had time to change out of her scrubs, she'd gotten a message to come back. She looked ragged enough without adding rumpled scrubs to the mix—three really hard days had left her with frizzy hair and perpetually tired-looking eyes—but she wanted the kid to get out too, and wasn't going to delay it by taking time to primp first.

Even if it meant avoiding eye contact with her former coworkers as she passed them en route to Jenna's room and repeating a prayer under her breath, like a mantra: *Don't let him see me. Don't let me see him.*

She didn't knock; the door was open, and Mrs. Lindsey was taking down the twinkle lights.

Made it in time.

"Dr. Angel!" Jenna chirruped upon seeing her, her color and cheer making Angel doubly glad she came. She wore actual pajamas instead of that awful hospital gown and was standing.

"Look at you!" Angel smiled, probably for the first time since Saturday, and gave the girl a gentle hug. "You must be doing what the doctors tell you—eating, taking your walks, using your spirometer for breathing exercises. And now making it home before Christmas, making my Christmas perfect."

Perfect.

"I am, and feel lots better." Jenna hugged her back, then shuffled to the wall to retrieve her rolling tray where her laptop sat. "I got you a present!"

"You got me a present?" Angel asked, slipping the small box she'd brought from her pocket as a focus—something tangible to keep her focus on what she was doing and how she was supposed to be behaving, a way to control her thoughts and keep them from drifting back to Wolfe. "I got you something too."

A handful of words, and Jenna instantly abandoned the computer, immediately shuffling back to claim the box, eyes widening as she whispered, "This is the size of jewelry boxes."

Angel wasn't giving any other Christmas presents; she'd enjoy this one. "It is about that size, isn't it?"

Jenna eased onto the edge of the bed, and at first it looked as if she was going to untie the ribbon with a delicate touch, but it took only a second before she began wrestling the small bit of satin from around the box. As soon as it was free, she opened the lid with such vigor the top flipped onto the floor and the rest of the box followed after she tumbled out the little velvet box inside.

"It *is* a jewelry box..." The velvet got a single swipe on her cheek, a tactile pleasure, and she flipped it open.

"What did Dr. Angel get you?" Mrs. Lindsey asked, picking up the dropped boxes while her daughter reached inside to straighten the small silver pendant on the delicate chain.

"It's an angel necklace."

To remember her by. Something to bear Angel's prayer for Jenna's recovery and remission. A piece of *something* to alleviate the crush of guilt that came with knowing she was abandoning her first patient.

"Do you know about the different angels? That's Michael, he's an archangel, a warrior. He never stops fighting for mankind," Angel explained, nothing left in her hands to distract from the guilt. She was never far from crying the past few days and didn't want to start now. Her keys in her pocket helped.

For a moment Jenna looked almost sad, but it passed in a second. "I want to wear it right now."

"Are you sure?" Angel asked, picking up on some level of hesitation.

Jenna handed the box to her mom to put it on her. "I just don't want Michael to be my replacement angel."

Because *she* was Jenna's angel.

"I know." Angel couldn't bring herself to say again that she was leaving. She just didn't have the heart. Especially after Mrs. Lindsey put the necklace on her daughter and Jenna reached up to press it into her neck, protectively covering it, almost embracing it with her hand. The same reverence that had kept Angel touching that dang beaded bag before she'd lost it. It was probably better for her sanity that she'd lost it.

"I'm glad you like it." Angel's voice wobbled. "And so happy for you that you get to go home today."

"Jen?"

Jenna looked at her mother, who carried the laptop.

"Don't you want to show Dr. Angel the video you made for her?"

Instantly, the girl's demeanor changed, and once again she was all smiles as she took the device.

"You made me a video?"

"Well, I helped." Jenna patted the bed beside her and started the video while Angel sat to watch, and Mrs. Lindsey began fiddling with her phone.

The video started with a round of the rooms and the children, many of whom had been her patients at one point, saying what they'd liked about the Christmas stories, as their videos had come to be called outside Wolfe's *shenanigans* moniker. Without the keys to worry, she'd have started crying at the second room, both because of the sweet things the children said, and maybe a little pride that she'd been able to give those smiles to them. Even proud that Wolfe had helped. It warmed her, but it also burned—being so reminded and always hearing their names linked.

Dr. Angel and Dr. Wolfe did this. Dr. Wolfe and Dr. Angel did that.

Tree. Skating. Cookies. Presents.

Presents? The first time that came up, she just smiled; kids always associated Christmas with presents. But about the fifth time, and with the mention of opening presents as something they looked forward to, she became alarmed.

There were no more activities scheduled. Alberts had let them be done after the ball, mostly because she'd barely contained her tears while begging to change shifts for her final weeks.

The video became footage of the hallway being traversed by wheelchair, and Jenna's voice narrating. "We're going to the activity room for a surprise."

Now? She looked at Jenna, who was smiling at her, her eyes so full of stars and happiness that Angel simply couldn't speak. Instead, she looked back at the video.

Inside the activities room, long bands of massive paper had been unrolled and affixed to the wall. Tables with cups of markers sat at regular intervals, and all over the paper were blocks of texts, little happy toddler scribbles, doodles of Christmas trees and presents. She didn't know what any of it was, but it felt like a gift. They'd made her a video as thank you or...

"I wrote this one," Jenna's voice announced from the video and it zoomed in on a block of neatly written blue text.

"What's it say?" another voice on the video asked.

Wolfe. It was Wolfe's voice. Her heart flopped out of rhythm twice, then began beating so hard and fast there was no way to slow her breathing, no way to hide her reaction.

Why was he involved? He wanted her to *leave*.

"'Dear Dr. Angel, we love you and don't want you to go. My mom said you can visit us, and it's okay because I have bunk beds. PS, my mom's a really good cook.'"

Key-fidgeting failed her. Biting the inside of her jaw, another technique she'd often used to control her emotions, also failed to dam the flood rising in her eyes.

The paper banners were for her. All of them. She didn't *have* that many people in her life to write words of encouragement.

"She'll appreciate that invitation, lass," said

video Wolfe. "Hand me the camera. I want to get some of the top up close, so she can read them."

Jenna pressed a tissue into her hand and leaned in to hug her arm, but said nothing. The change in elevation and some rattling showed the camera being handed off to someone taller.

Wordlessly, he walked, scanning the blocks of text, fast enough to show the numbers but she couldn't read more than a few words here and there.

Until he zoomed in on one, a name she recognized—the parent of a patient she'd seen and admitted last week, thanking her for her dedication and having the heart to treat their spirits as well as their bodies.

Her chest squeezed hard, and she clamped her mouth shut to keep silent the sob she'd felt coming but couldn't stop. Quietly crying in front of a patient was bad enough, even when the kid had had a hand in orchestrating it, but losing her mind and having a breakdown was too far.

Was this him trying to give her a kind farewell? To make her feel better before she left? Something to ease the ache?

He moved on, spot-shooting different messages while others flew by in a blur of colorful handwriting.

Coworkers, lamenting not having known her before the videos. What they'd miss, not having her around. Thoughtful and unscripted, like genuine praise, genuine compliments. *Reasons to stay.* Which would mean he couldn't, he'd said.

Even Lyons had signed. No sentimental words, he just wrote: *A good doctor is always missed, Lyons McKeag.*

"Mine's not on here, lass," Wolfe said softly, and Angel knew he was speaking to her before he turned the camera around. "I messed up. Don't think I could have enough room to write my apology if I had all these papers to myself. Been doin' a lot of thinking, and all I know for sure is this can't be the end. If you go, I'll go with you. My malfunctioning robot half worked out the programming error. Turned out it was a number problem. Ones and zeros don't work when you were made to be one of two."

He took a breath, his gaze falling for a moment, but he kept the camera on himself, documenting it, showing her the struggle as he composed himself, and when he lifted his beautiful eyes again she saw dampness. And enough regret to fill an ocean. Tingling erupted all over her body, a lightness so powerful she'd swear she was about to astral project if she believed in that nonsense.

Where was he? Was he coming?

She didn't want to look away from the screen, but had to look at the door, to check.

"I realized where I went wrong," he said after too long a pause. "It wasn't easy to talk to you because I couldn't mess you up if I was meaningless. That's what I thought, that it was easy to talk to you as long as you weren't important to me. But you became important to me that night at the rink. I didn't realize it until I messed up, and nearly lost my mind trying to figure out how to fix it. You were never supposed to be mine, and I told myself that meant I was free to relax and not worry. But when you felt like you *were* mine, it got harder to talk—not because I was afraid of hurting you, but because I was afraid of *losing* you. Then I pushed you away because I'm a damn fool."

His smile, rueful and lopsided, made the words possibly real. "I think I need you to talk it through with me, so I understand why I do the things I do. I always think I know, but I'm starting to doubt much of what I think I know."

As apologies went, it was the best thing she'd ever heard, even before he said, "There's more.

I'll tell you everything, but I need to say one thing that can't wait. I love you. That's not changing, doesn't matter where you want to live. Everyone here wants you to stay, but if you can't, I'll go with you. Even if you want to go to Scotland and live under the shadow of the infamous, scandalous McKeag name."

She hit pause, the words rushing over her in a way that almost hurt. Was that a proposal?

That sounded a lot like a proposal.

Or was it just the shadow that would cover him to her by close association?

It couldn't be a proposal. It couldn't be that good, that easy. Nothing had ever come that easily. She'd worked hard for everything she achieved. And she wanted this more than she'd ever wanted.

She needed to see him in person. She needed to hear his voice without the wires and bits transmitting it to her. It was the only way to stop her heart from exploding with hope. She grabbed her new phone and scrambled, looking for his number.

"Dr. Angel?" Mrs. Lindsey said her name, placed a hand over the phone and urged it down. "Watch the rest. It's not much longer."

Watch the rest? She needed to breathe, but that

couldn't happen while she hung in this space between fear and knowing.

Still, she bumped play again.

"The kids and I prepared what I hope is a good apology." He turned the camera away from himself and toward the wall she'd not seen, which was lined with children, waiting so patiently, smiling and quiet. And a dress form holding the most godawful adult-sized princess dress she'd ever seen. "I ruined the ball, Cinderella. I don't have your shoe, but I've got this."

He moved the beaded bag in frame, resting in his open palm, then shifted the camera back to himself.

"We're in the activity room, and I owe you a proper dance. If you'll come dance with me."

The video stopped, holding his pale blue gaze directly to the camera, ensuring she'd never mistake or forget the hope and love she saw there, and the fear. The fear she'd been rolling in at the ball. The fear she'd never leave him alone with, not when she could help it.

She stood, looked at Jenna and Mrs. Lindsey, who were both crying with her, but didn't need to speak.

"We'll be right behind you," Mrs. Lindsey said, grabbing the wheelchair to load Jenna.

It felt rude not to wait. Wrong and rude and not something a civilized person would do, but she was already in the hallway, running for the activities room.

Her shoes squealed as she skidded to a stop in the doorway, and all eyes swiveled to her. The children and their parents sat just where they'd been shown. How long had they been waiting?

Different clothes, her mind supplied. Many were in different pajamas, which meant they'd done the filming yesterday, and gotten up early today to see it finish.

Wolfe walked into view, stopping in the center of the room. She met his gaze across the space, but she'd already made her decision before she'd even finished watching Jenna's video.

He waited, not pushing, not doing anything but watching her, waves of relief and happiness rolling off him so thick she'd swear she could see it, like disturbance in the air, heat rolling off a new fire to warm a cold, empty room.

Still no words came from either of them. Even once she'd started moving again. His arms came out, spread and welcoming, a promise to hold, to hug and to dance… The light in his eyes promised more.

She ran the last few paces and didn't stop until she'd collided with him and he'd pressed her teary face into the safety of his neck.

He tilted his head to whisper, "God, I was afraid you wouldn't come."

She laughed a little, uncaring how many people were watching or knew their business, even how many of them cared about the two of them—and judging by the clapping, they all did. "I was sure you wouldn't want me to."

"We're going to need more faith in one another." He didn't sound scolding, just like Wolfe—ever a little bit amused, even in intense situations.

"I've got another fear," he whispered into her hair.

"What is it?" She pulled back enough to look at him. What she really wanted was to kiss him, but the kids were there...

"You're going to have to wear that dress and dance with me before they're going to agree to going back to bed."

It was her turn to laugh then and she swiped her tears away when she saw him reaching for her cheeks to do it.

"If you did it, there would've been more," she

whispered to the flash of uncertainty she saw in his eyes. Just a flash, and she doubted anyone else would've seen it, but she'd seen behind his wall. She knew where the holes were now.

A moment later, they walked to the dress and a couple of the mothers came to help her put it over her scrubs, which of course made it just that much uglier. Clearly an adult princess costume, the poufy iridescent blue volume of the skirt was supported by some kind of filler that managed to itch even through her thick cotton scrubs.

Wolfe played his most charming, taking her hand and leading her to the floor while someone started music from an unseen music station. He apologized for that too, close at her ear. "I asked for something classic. They insisted that the puppet Christmas song was classic."

He tried to lead in a waltz, but that just wasn't happening with the raucous, tambourine-heavy music blasting through the activities room and the off-key kiddie voices singing along, never mind her complete inability to waltz—something she suddenly knew she wanted to remedy. Just to dance with him.

Laughing, both of them, he folded her closer,

adopting something closer to a high-school dance sway as he looked into her eyes. "I'm going to assume you want to be with me."

"Good assumption," she said, then asked, "What changed your mind?"

He looked momentarily chagrined and admitted, "Lyons said something, the negative mirror of what you'd done, and I heard the wrongness in his words."

"What was it?" She might have to change her mind about Lyons, even if he only *accidentally* helped them get back together.

"Lyons said, 'We're broken, and there's no fixing it. We are what they made us, and some other rotten misfortune,'" Wolfe said, then added, "And you basically said, these are my broken pieces, can you accept them? Not change them. Not make me into something else. Accept them. And I knew you'd already accepted my own broken pieces. But I hadn't."

She glanced to the children, not sure she could keep from crying again, but there was no way for her to stop this whispered conversation. "You hadn't accepted mine?"

"No, lass," he said softly, "I hadn't accepted *mine*. You had. It wasn't until the next day that

I realized the wrongness of the other bit he'd said. That there was no fixing it. Because there is. I'm learning how to be with you. I'm committed to it. To you. And I want you to see that you already know how to be here. How much you're wanted here. Not just by me, but, my God, if no one else wanted you, I'd spend every breath making sure to fill up any spaces left in your heart. And make a new family to replace the broken ones that made us."

Her lower lip wobbled and she squeezed tighter to him even as the music reached the cacophony of the bridge.

"I spoke with Alberts," he added, and she heard the worry in his voice, the same fear she felt rumbling her insides. "And a lawyer."

"A lawyer?" She focused on that first, pulling back to meet his gaze again.

"You have a case against your former employer. Your record was expunged. There is no documentation to back it up. No legal footing for firing you," he said. "And Alberts agreed. Did they actually say that you were fired?"

She replayed the final conversation in her mind, words that had been burned into her that day. "No. He more talked about how embarrassing it would be for me to stay, and that they were doing me a favor. I could go somewhere else with a clean slate."

He'd played on her insecurities, and she'd taken it and run, accepted that she'd deserved that exactly. And judging by the banners on the wall, the words of encouragement and support, she was still doing it.

Wolfe's arms tightened, "If that's how you feel if it ever comes out here, after I'm done crackin' heads, we can go. Or we can go now, somewhere you feel more secure. You don't have to deal with that while you're learnin' to feel secure with me."

"I already feel secure with you," she whispered.

He grinned then, eyes warm, and a little red, she noticed. She'd not been the only one suffering. "Where shall we be livin', then?"

"Church house," she whispered in his ear, then added, "but I want you to insure the breakables. Really."

"There are no breakables worth extra insurance."

"Appliances, then."

He laughed softly, as was his way. "Fine, they're already insured as part of the house, but consider the request met."

She looked over at the wall and the paper covering it, really getting an idea of the scope of the messages left for her in person. "How did you do all this?"

"I put up the paper in the staff room in Emergency for two days and brought it up here in the evenings so you were unlikely to see it. Asked people to sign your going-away banner."

"You didn't tell them to write nice things?"

"No, love. I told them to write a message if they wanted."

Her eyes started to sting again; she had to look away.

"Don't do that," he whispered. "You don't have to hide."

"Oh, I'm just crying because I don't want to go to work later," she teased, because she knew he knew better.

"I already called off for the day." He stuck his tongue out.

"Brat."

"Yep." He squeezed closer. "But I reckon we could take those stitches out, and I'll write you a doctor's note to get you off."

They were ready, but, more importantly, *she* was ready. Not for the stitches, though that would be nice, but to be alone with him. Thankfully, the puppet song ended, and their dance with it. They took a few minutes to talk to the kids, made promises that Santa would be coming soon and said their goodbyes.

"I've got several hours before my shift starts," she whispered, taking his hand and turning to smile as the last child rolled out, leaving them alone. "Do we have to stay and clean up? Because I'd really like you to take me home."

He turned her into his arms as soon as the door swung closed, his tender, loving kiss melting the last bit of ice that had settled in her chest on the night of the ball.

Something bulky in his jacket pocket thumped against her frumpy-dress-covered hip and she pulled back enough to look down.

"I almost forgot." The look in his eyes contradicted him, but he feigned casualness while dipping his hand into his pocket to fetch the peacock clutch, which he handed to her. It had something lumpy in it. And not shaped like her phone. Or her keys.

She flipped open the clasp and peeked inside. Nestled in the deep blue silk was an iconic pale blue box with a white bow. "Wolfe…"

"Don't open it," he said quickly. "I want you

to wait to open it until you're ready. But when you're ready, I'll have words to say too."

Another promise, in case she hadn't quite understood the first one, or maybe in case she hadn't quite believed it. Not leaving anything to chance.

She nodded, kissed him and asked again, "Take me home?"

Late that night, long after she should've reported for her shift—which Alberts had amiably canceled for her in exchange for rescinding her resignation—she opened the box while Wolfe lay beautiful and bare, stretched out asleep on the bed beside her.

Inside sat a gorgeous square diamond on an intricately carved band, glittering more than the Christmas tree she'd been pleased to see he'd finished on his own.

Placing the small box on his chest, she leaned in to whisper into his sleeping ear, "I want you to say your words."

He came awake immediately, a smile on his sleepy face, arm around her shoulders contracting to keep her against him.

He spoke of his hopes for their future—children, triumphs and holidays in the snow—but he also spoke about what worried him, so open and unfiltered it sounded like poetry to someone who knew far too much about surviving bad times alone. The promise of someone to survive bad times with, to share grief with, was beautiful, and brought a kind of peace she'd never even known existed.

It also carried the promise of this being a Christmas to remember, even if neither of them knew what they were doing.

"I want to keep doing all the things until Christmas gets here." she said.

His brows popped up, but he smiled. "After Santa comes are you going to wear the elf costume for me?"

"I thought I just got a promotion to Mrs. Claus?"

"Okay, okay. Wear the elf costume for me later though." He wiggled his brows before tugging her in for a kiss. "I was promised lots of amazing, crazy sex."

"I didn't say crazy."

"Elf sex."

"I didn't say elf sex." She laughed at the fool. "Well, okay. But I get kilted Highland warrior sex since my stitches are out."

He chuckled and rolled, "I'll get my kilt." His warm, firm length pressed her into the mattress on the side with her *good* knee and stopped all their silly bartering with a much more serious kiss that would last until dawn.

* * * * *

LET'S TALK

Romance

For exclusive extracts, competitions
and special offers, find us online:

f facebook.com/millsandboon

⦿ @millsandboonuk

🐦 @millsandboon

Or get in touch on 0844 844 1351*

For all the latest titles coming soon,
visit millsandboon.co.uk/nextmonth